—At night the moaning again. Dear God, I thought I'd have peace this evening. I want to read. I thought I'd read alone in my room. Better alone than prattling in the drawing room. But now it's Claire again, that sound she makes, the sound of it so clear I might imagine myself in their bedroom . . .—

Blue Tango

BLUE TANGO

ANONYMOUS

BLUE MOON BOOKS
NEW YORK

Published by
Blue Moon Books
841 Broadway, Fourth Floor
New York, NY 10003

ISBN 1-56201-178-2

Manufactured in the United States of America

All life is a dream, and dreams are dreams.
Pedro Calderon De La Barca
(1600–1681)

Part One: Julie

Chapter One

Now the noise again, the moaning, the pleading in her voice. Is she pleading? I can't imagine it. I lie here bereft. In the darkness. No, the room is not dark, the room is grey. The moonlight filters through the window, through the windowpanes, the curtains, the grey moonlight hanging like a cloud over the shapes in the room. Is that my hat? Yes, of course it's the large hat I wore on Wednesday, the pale green hat that looked so pretty in the park. Everyone liked it. They smiled at me. Oh, they didn't smile, don't be silly. You're acting like a twit, darling. It's the moaning. She hasn't stopped. It goes on and on. I want to drum on the walls. I shall beg her to stop it. I won't allow it. Well, you can't do much about allowing things, can you? You ought to sleep, darling. It's a beastly hour and you ought to sleep. And her? Please God let me sleep. I can't bear it, I really can't bear it.

I suppose it's possible for me to keep myself in a state of utter immobility. I shall lie here like a mummy while she moans in the next room. I shall lie here with my hands upon my breasts. Holding my breasts. I must hold my breasts or I shall certainly go mad. How strange it is to hear the sound of it. Or perhaps it's not strange at all. I ought to consider the nature of things, the proper aspects. In any case, I thought this room would be lovely and it's not lovely at all. Lovely in the day and not lovely at night. Not lovely to have her beyond that wall. Thank God the bed is not against that wall. But I ought to have it there because of the window. I don't like a bed near a window and that's where I have the bed now. No, it's not where I have the bed, it's where the bed was situated when I was given the room. Darling, you don't want the bed moved. You can't possibly want the bed against that wall. That's completely out of the question, completely impossible.

And Edward? Not a sound to betray his presence. He's there of course. One can't help the imagining. No sound but the sound of Claire, yet Edward is certainly there. In connubial extension. The wet coupling. Really, darling. How does he hold her? You shouldn't, you really shouldn't. But of course it's not possible to do otherwise. I can't lie here like a stone. I am not a stone. I imagine she lies on her back with her legs raised. She's quite limber. She rides well. She dances well. She does everything well. Now Edward is riding her. Like Sir Lancelot with his sturdy lance thrusting in and out of the quick. His cock in her nest. I wonder if it's dark in there. I wonder if they fancy the electric lamp. Claire might but I'm sure Edward wouldn't. Edward is much too modest. He would have his thrusting in the dark. Nothing to see. Everything to hear and nothing to see. Softly now. The moaning is soft again. The sounds of pleasure in Claire's throat. My hands upon my breasts. The fullness of my breasts. My nipples. The grey fog of moonlight in a darkened room.

* * *

"Did you sleep well?"

Claire is so sparkling in the morning, so fresh and perfect. We sit at the breakfast table, Edward between Claire and myself, the servants gliding around us, the April sunlight vibrating through the glass of the French window. Claire and Edward and myself.

"Yes, quite well, thank you."

"And your room? Do you like your room, Julie?"

"Yes, of course."

"Well, not of course. You might have another, you know. This isn't the largest house in London but we do have other rooms. I'm sure we can find something suitable."

"But the room is fine."

"I thought you might like to be near us."

"Yes, I like that."

"It's a cool room in summer."

Edward rustles his newspaper. "I don't think we'll be here."

"What?"

"I said I don't think we'll be here in the midst of summer. I should think we'd be abroad."

"Ah yes. Will you like that, Julie? You shall come with us, of course. We'll speak French again, won't we, darling?"

"Yes, I think I'd like that very much."

"And not a motorcar, Edward. I don't want any motoring in France this year. I don't like it."

"As you wish."

Claire smiles at me. "He likes to dash about on the roads."

Edward puts his newspaper down. "I don't dash about."

"Men must have their amusements."

Edward grumbles. "You close your eyes, my dear."

"Close my eyes to what?"

"To the advance of civilization."

"Oh dear. I think we need more tea. Another pot, Dobbin, and some sugar, please."

The maid flies. All the maids fly when Claire has need of them. Edward stirs his tea, his face grey, his eyes so completely empty.

Then the maid returns, the blonde Dobbin, the

girl who brought my chocolate in the morning. A pot of tea on a silver tray, the color high in her cheeks. As she leans forward to place the pot upon the table, Edward extends his hand to cup the bulging of her bottom.

The girl hesitates a moment. A blush in her cheeks. Then the pot is placed and her back is straight again. Edward's hand hasn't moved. It moves now. A circular movement as he strokes the maid's curving rear.

"She's my favorite," Edward savs. "The prettiest of the lot."

Claire makes a sound of disapproval. "I don't think so. I think Larkin is much the prettier."

Edward chuckles. "Well, yes, I suppose they're a pair. But this one has the nicer bottom. And more capability. I don't think women appreciate the importance of capability. One can have them bending nicely to be corked, but it's what they do with it once they have it that counts. Turn, Dobbin, lift your skirts."

Claire is annoyed. "Edward, not here."

Edward ignores her. The girls turns. Her plain black dress, her grey petticoat pulled and raised, one hand still holding the silver tray. Her black cotton stockings and milk-white thighs. She wears no drawers, nothing to cover the white bulging orbs and the deep split between. She has a strong bottom, the curving prominent, the flesh firm. Edward dips his fingers in the plate of marmalade and carefully works them between the girl's nether-cheeks.

Dobbin groans.

"Easy, Dobbin. Lean forward a bit."

She leans forward. Her bottom protruding. I can see his fingers in her bottom-hole, the stretching of the ring. She moves her legs apart. Her black cotton stockings. She arches her back a bit more. Edward's fingers are sliding. Two fingers in and out of the maid's fundament. The girl moans. I see only part of her face, her closed eyes, the glistening of sweat upon her brow. Her mouth hangs open and from the hanging jaws come the bleating sounds of her submission.

He makes her spend. One can see it in the shivering, the wobbling of her legs. She pulls his fingers out of the sucking grasp of her bottom, wipes his hands with a cloth napkin and tosses the napkin at the floor.

"She's a healthy wench. They don't spend so easily when they're not healthy."

* * *

In the afternoon I lie upon the bed in my room. Dear Claire. Dear sister Claire. Èdward is so quaint. Like a dusty old deacon in one of the cellars in Canterbury. The way he fondled that maid. His fingers in her bottom. Well, she did like it, didn't she? One time with John at that awful house in Royston. His aunt in the drawing room and the two of us upstairs in our whisperings. Beware of the old aunt down below. She's a witch, John said. He had his thumb in my bottom-hole. He liked to use his thumb in my bottom-hole and the other fingers tickling my quim. He had me standing, my skirts raised like the maid Dobbin, his thumb corking my bottom-hole while he stroked my clitoris. I liked it. I do like it. I like their fingers. They get so helpless when you let them at you. We had to whisper because the house was so old and the floor had a grate. Then John was on the floor and I straddled him to take his lordship in her ladyship. Giggling as I danced.

There was a time when I spoke nothing but

French. I lived in Paris with my parents in a cluttered house. All those rooms. Claire was already married to Edward, in England with her English husband, all her dolls left behind in an old trunk in the attic. I was still a child, still uncertain of things. My mother would read the letters from Claire. Her days with Edward and his family. The parties in Mayfair. I was overwhelmed with envy. You shall have your turn, my mother said. One day you too shall have a husband.

I pull the cord to summon a maid. Will it be Dobbin? Yes, it's Dobbin. She still has the color in her cheeks.

"Yes, madam?"

"I'd like a bath drawn. Can I have that?"

"Yes, madam, I'll have it done."

"And you might help me."

"Yes, madam."

The girl returns before long.

"What's your Christian name?"

"Nellie, madam."

"That's a nice name."

"Thank you, madam." She begins to undress me.

"You spent on his fingers this morning, didn't you? On the master's fingers."

Pink cheeks and a lowering of her eyes. "Yes, madam."

"His fingers in your bottom."

She says nothing. I am down to chemise and stockings. I lift my foot and she rolls one stocking down. Then the other foot. Then my chemise. I stand naked before the cheval glass and hold my breasts in my hands. "How old are you?"

"Eighteen, madam."

Her eyes are upon my copse, the bush of curls beneath my belly. "Do you want to kiss it?"

The flushing of her throat. "Madam?"

"Yes you do. Come on, then. We'll find out how clever you are."

I like to be kind to them. Clever she is and clever she does. She kneels at my feet, presses her face against my belly. Her nose in the curls. The hot kissing at my copse. I push her down a bit, open my legs to straddle her face. "Well, that's better. Kiss it now." In a moment I drizzle upon her mouth, her nose rubbing at my clitoris as she takes my spending.

"My dressing gown, Nellie. I can't walk in the corridor like this, can I?"

* * *

And at night the moaning again. Dear God, I thought I'd have peace this evening. I want to read. I thought I'd read alone in my room. Better alone than prattling in the drawing room. But now it's Claire again, that sound she makes, the sound of it so clear I might imagine myself in their bedroom.

They ought to have given me another room. I don't want this burden. It's madness. How indulgent she is. One can hear the indulgence in the way she moans. This enormous house that Edward has provided. Her clothes. Well, you might be envious, darling. No, I'm not envious. Not of that. I don't like her taste in clothes. Her kid boots. She's a bit old-fashioned, isn't she? I'd want the money to buy other things. In Paris. I'd buy so many things in Paris. Then you're envious, indeed. Yes, I'm envious. What a sniggering little sin that is. Does it make me awful? Must I do penance for my envy? I envy Claire the possession of a husband with a large income. There, my secret is uncovered. I have no husband at all, not any more. John is not here any more. John is lost somewhere. No, he's not lost, darling, he's drowned in the Channel and dead. They found the balloon, didn't they? Drowned like a young puppy. Well, that's what he was, a young puppy. Such a lovely fool. Not like Edward at all. Edward is a fool in his own way, but he's not lovely. Does Claire find him lovely? Perhaps she does at the moment. That moaning. Sometimes it's a whimper. Oh, the sound of it will drive me mad. It was so kind of her to ask me to live here, but the sound of it will drive me mad. But you're cheating, darling. You can't deny it's exciting. To hear them at it. The doings in that room. Claire's bedroom. He goes to his own afterward. He leaves the bed and goes to his own room and shuts the door. I heard the door close last night. Edward having finished his connubial engagement.

Now the creaking. Dear God, what are they up to? And she's laughing. It's not fair that I'm the one to be alone. She's eight years older and it's the older one who ought to be alone. Oh, that's nasty. That's quite nasty, darling. I want to break that Chinese vase. I want to break the vase against the wall. Give them a turn, wouldn't it? I should think Claire would lose her senses. Now the creaking again. Is she riding him now? Or is it Edward who rides? One never knows who does the riding. The way he fingered the maid at breakfast. Does he do that to Claire? Darling, you're acting a bit wild. Rubbing my nipples. Yes. And down there too. The wetness. One can't help rubbing it. Does he have the maids? Yes, of course, he has the maids. He has the maids and he has Claire. My lovely sister has his thrusting and I'm envious. His cock thrusting. His balls. His hands holding her bottom. John liked to hold my bottom. The slapping of his balls against my quim. The slapping of Edward's balls. I must go on. My wet fingers. How awful it is to have wet fingers.

Chapter Two

BREAKFAST WITH CLAIRE. The two of us are alone this morning. White lace curtains, the bright morning sun. The maids flit about in silence.

Claire smiles. "You look unhappy, darling."

"I'm not unhappy."

"Well, I don't like to see you sad. I shouldn't like that, should I?"

She flutters her agile fingers. I want to flee. I want to fly away through the open window. I shall be a bird in a tree, a silly bird singing a silly song.

There is nothing here, not a sound except the tinkling of cup and saucer. Outside a soft rustling in the trees and an occasional chirp. Claire smiles and flutters her fingers in the silence. I fumble with my toast. The memories of last night. The groaning.

I am more curvaceous than Claire, more breast and buttock. Claire is unfashionably thin. She has an ethereal quality that I have always envied. She was always thin. She remains thin. She disdains plumpness.

Now again these disastrous images. Again and again I construct the tableau. Her legs surrounding his, her toes in the air. But of course one never knows the hidden things. Her eyes. The way she smiles at him. The showing of her small, perfect teeth. John always said Claire hardly smiled enough. He said she was too grim. But I don't see the grimness. She's not at all grim. She certainly wasn't grim last night. In the dark? Well, of course, if they do it in the dark then Edward can hardly see her smile at him. If she does smile. If she does hold him with her legs. Edward surrounded by her legs in the dark. The bed creaking, creaking. I do hate it when the bed creaks. Does he kiss her while the bed creaks? Does he mutter? I imagine Edward mutters.

"Oh dear, there's a fly in the room."

The maid scurries. Perkin, the dark one. Claire frowns, her eyes following the trails of the maid. The fly has fortitude. Perkin is sweating. Then at last the fly is smashed and Perkin flushes in her victory.

Claire is amused. She calls Perkin, turns her chair to the side. "Kiss my shoe."

The maid is obedient. The girl kneels, bends, her lips touching the tip of Claire's shoe. Claire smiles and sends the girl away.

"She's clumsy at times. I don't like to have them clumsy. Tell me your plan."

"Plan?"

"For the day, silly. How will you spend your day?"

"I hadn't thought of it."

"Then come with me. We must have the air this afternoon."

"I don't know why."

"It's a question of health, Julie. Darling, you look so pale. We shall drive in the park."

"Which park?"

"St. James's, of course. The others are a bore."

"I thought I would look at some shops."

"Well, you might do that afterward."

She insists. I must drive with her in the park. After all, I am here and I must do something. At the moment I have no interest in the park. My interest is a stupid obsession concerning the entanglement of Claire and Edward on that bed in her room. How awful of me. You're a silly bird, darling. You ought to be out there with the other birds. You ought to be out there chirping among the leaves. Were the sea birds watching when John fell into the Channel?

* * *

All the parks are boring and St. James's Park is truly the worst. A competition of hats. The sun flickering through the trees. The blank faces. Empty glances from carriage to carriage. Claire prattling about a dressmaker. "I've always had a passion for ribbons." Her hand covers mine. "We shall make you happy."

Do I want to be happy? Yes, I suppose I do. I would like to be out of this park. She pats my hand. The sunlight hurts my eyes. I ought to repin my hat. Claire comments about each carriage we pass. She talks of nothing but hats and ribbons. She pats my hand and talks of ribbons. "We shall make you happy, darling. We shall make you quite happy."

I think of the days that are no more. Claire and I as children. Old Mathilde in her kitchen. The smell of burnt wood in the morning. Mother and her needlework. The absent-minded kisses. The twisted staircase. The red plush draperies. The gold Italian madonna brought by Father from Venice. Claire liked to tease me in the evening when we prayed alone in our room. Mother would look at the fireplace before she left us, though the painted pottery on the shelf over the small table. Pottery bowls and pottery angels. Claire and I giggling in the darkening room. I think of John again, that time in Folkestone when he had me giggling on the beach. I could see his cods in his bathing suit. He swore I could not but I really could. The bulge of his ballocks. In the evening I held them in my hand as I sucked his plum.

After the drive, Claire and I have tea and cakes in a shop in Regent Street. A throng of hats in a room of crowded tables. The ladies gawking at each other like surprised pheasants. Claire is always amused. "That one looks awful."

"Which?"

"That pink hat. Pink and green. All that nonsense on the brim. It's quite ugly, don't you think?"

"She's an old woman."

"They're all old. I won't come back here any more."

How impatient she is. Her fingers turning the cup. Her think body. Does Edward enjoy his women lean? I imagine them naked beside each other on her bed. The white flesh of their bodies. Flesh against flesh. Edward's affair like a pink stalk in her hand. Does she perfume her copse?

Do I love Claire? We have the bond of common flesh, the years of awakening. The years of competition for the pretty dress. The jealousies during the walks on Sundays. Is Claire in my image? No, we are not alike. We have our separate satisfactions. And Edward can be so dreary. I abhor the vacancy of a smug life in Kensington. I would like to tease Edward. I want to rub my hand along his skin. I want to hold his penis in my hand. He will mutter at me, smile and mutter, his face always empty of emotion. One can feel the tremor in his cock, the hot blood of a man's attention. Does he press his lips against Claire's neck when he spends? Does he whisper against her cheek? Sometimes Edward's eyes show his puzzlement. He watches Claire without understanding. He looks at me for guidance. Are we not sisters?

I do not think much of Edward's idleness. In the evening he turns the pages of a dull weekly. He says nothing. Claire talks and talks, but Edward says nothing. When spoken to directly, he turns another page as he mumbles his reply. How awful it is. I want to throw something. John was the same. His cigar in the evening and his pompous silence. Was he silent when his balloon was blown away by the wind? I don't want to look at these ladies. Some day I shall arrive in Paris and find the place cluttered with English tea shops. I would like to stroll in Oxford Street but of course Claire will refuse. I like to linger. I like to watch people at work. The men. The smells of the horses as they pass in the road. Sometimes a man will ask me to come with him. A silly man with pink cheeks.

My father had pink cheeks and whiskers. A smell of tobacco in his hair. His waistcoat bulging under the chain of his gold watch. We laughed in the garden. He whispered secrets to us and we laughed. Mother chided him. She said his shoes were dusty. Father would laugh and press against her, coaxing her with his hands. Claire liked to flutter at his coattails. Father would stroke Claire, then he would look at me and smile.

Outside the teashop, Claire leaves me. "Don't be late, darling. I shall send the carriage for you in an hour."

The horse looks tired. Claire waves at me as they drive off. In a moment she's gone and I walk to Oxford Street. I enjoy the bustle, the people crowding the walk. I enjoy my isolation. I am alone. I am content. I wear grey kid boots and my dress is in fashion. In Oxford Circus, a man wearing a brown derby smiles at me from his carriage. He wishes me to join him. I turn my eyes away. I imagine his breath upon my neck. John liked me to expose my breasts in his presence. He would have me stand in my chemise, and then I would drop my chemise to my waist to bare my breasts. I want to bare my breasts now to the gentleman in the brown derby. I want to show my swollen nipples, the white skin of my breasts. I want to see the passion in his eyes. He reaches for me but I push his hands away. He is not to touch me. Not yet. I have my own amusements. He smiles with understanding as he unbuttons his flies. His penis appears. His pink cock. He pulls at his foreskin to uncover his bulb. Then a great shudder courses through him as he spouts his essence into the dust of the road. The carriage is behind me now. When I turn, I see nothing but the brown derby hat above the folded awning.

I walk in Oxford Street. I look at the shop windows. The crowd hums around me. A hawker selling ribbons calls out to me with a red band of silk. Ladies walk in pairs. How amusing it is when they look at me and wonder who I am. These tedious people. Now in a carriage a man in a Chesterfield and a woman in blue. The windows of the shops are too ordinary. I avoid the eyes of the carriages now. I turn away when someone looks at me. I think John ought to have done more with his life than sail in his balloon. He ought to have done something. Now I have nothing but fading images and the sounds of my sister in her bedroom.

After a while I walk to Regent Street again and there I turn in to a print shop. It's a musty old place with Italian engravings and photographs of cathedrals in bins against the walls. The people in the shop whisper at each other. Someone chuckles as I finger my way through a stack of prints. The dust is thick. In another bin I find an ugly photograph of a church in Devonshire. I can't imagine who would want such a thing. Do they look at me? I think of that week with John in Cambridge. How we whispered in the gray light. That room at the inn. The window. He had me at the window, my shirts raised, my body bent, his penis full up my bottom as the dons walked by in the yard below.

"I'd like something of London Bridge," a woman says. She hangs on the arm of a man in plaid. She squints at the clerk. She wears a large yellow hat with white flowers clustered on the crown and around the rim. Undoubtedly the man in plaid is her husband. She has the appearance of a wide bottom and on occasion he takes her there. His corker churning deep in her fundament. As she bends. A quiver in her throat as she feels the spending. Essentially feminine. The important act is the act of penetration. One wants the pego thick and hard. The fullness of the entry produces a tense emotional state. Perhaps not in every woman. One never knows about every woman. But in this woman who asks for a drawing of London Bridge. She has a lover she visits at his offices in the City. She enjoys a particular state of mind, the quiverings of a woman in the midst of surrender. John said I enjoyed my moments of surrender. My turmoil. Those delicate explosions in my marrow. My body trembling in his arms. I was often hungry for it, hungry for the sweetness of it, hungry for his kisses. Frenzied claspings upon a velvet chaise. His hands upon my breasts. The questing. My nipples stroked by his fingers. His fingers in my nest. His fingers upon my clitoris. That perfect caress. I moan. I arch my body to his fingers. I beg him not to stop. The fingers insistent. Oh, you silly girl, you mustn't think of it. How stupid to tremble here in a musty old print shop in Oxford Street. John would be amused. He once bought an engraving of Chartres for me. In this shop? How amusing that John bought the print of Chartres in this very shop.

Quite, darling. How very amusing. And on the day John went down in that lovely red and white balloon, it was Arthur Stockton who held you in his arms. On the velvet chaise, wasn't it? Yes, of course, you do remember. Arthur's whiskers against my throat as John descended in his balloon like a plumb-line to the deeps of the Channel. Reggie Cooper calculated the time of descent as something more than two minutes. I don't think Arthur's poke lasted that long, but one ought to assume it did and that the events were contemporaneous. John descending to the deeps of the Channel and Arthur Stockton spouting in the deeps of John's wife. One remembers the trivial things. I remember the disarray, my dress thrown back, my legs pushed wide apart on each side of the chaise. And Arthur's tweed. Or was it something striped? No, I think it was tweed. The only man apart from John to have me on that chaise.

They are all gone, no one but the clerk and myself in the print shop now. I buy a framed photograph of Ellen Terry. The clerk assures me Miss Terry is one of the finest actresses of our time. Her chin is raised in the photograph. Is she looking at the heavens? Darling, why Ellen Terry? I don't know. I really don't know. I don't like statues any more. Photographs like this one seem more to the point. One yields to the ministrations of memory. I take the parcel. I shudder as the clerk's hand accidentally touches mine. I am like a child. I have no thought beyond the pleasure of that moment. John often said it. He would say it to me when he made love to me on the velvet chaise. Arthur Stockton never said anything of the sort. Poor Arthur was really much too quick. Something more than two minutes is really much too quick.

I walk now in Oxford Street with Ellen Terry. I shall take down those insipid roses in my room and replace them with one of the finest actresses of our time. She does look so stupid staring at the heavens like that. Thankfully her eyes are not turned outward. I don't like to be stared at by people in photographs. I don't like the accusing eyes. One can imagine them thinking anything. I shall think of Arthur Stockton whenever I look at Ellen Terry. Yes, of course, how fit that is. I shall think of Arthur Stockton, and whenever I think of Arthur Stockton I shall think of John descending in his balloon to the Channel.

Claire's driver finds me in front of the teashop in Regent Street. I carry Ellen Terry with me as I return home. I feel drenched in the aftermath of a wicked afternoon. All those people. The eyes looking at me. The imaginings. Ellen Terry's dreamy face. I did see her once at the Criterion. Now I shall see her constantly.

Claire greets me at the door. "Lovely time?"

"Yes, it was pleasant."

"Tell Dobbin when you want to bathe."

"Yes, I will."

She continues talking as I climb the stairs. I don't want to talk any more. All these years of talking. There's no point to it, is there? Inside my bedroom, I close the door and immediately attack the insipid roses, the painting on the wall between my room and Claire's room. A chair. A step upon the chair. I reach for the roses, unhook the frame. I bring the roses down. When I raise my eyes again, I see the grate.

The moment stands isolated, frozen, my throat constricted. I am not at all certain I want to see it. A grate in the wall. A grate high up in the wall between my room and Claire's, hidden all this time by those horrible roses. I don't want to think about it. I have a fierce passion not to think about it. I turn and stare at the photograph of Ellen Terry already unwrapped upon the bed. My face is warm. Oh darling. Yes, you will. You know you will. I stand upon the chair. My eyes at the grate. Claire's room uncovered in the soft light of dusk. And the bed. Nearly all the room so easily seen. I step down. I take the photograph of Ellen Terry and step up again. I cover the grate and step down again. Down and up and down again like a mindless automation. I refused to think of it. I bury the roses beneath my bed. I ring for Dobbin to draw my bath.

Chapter Three

CLAIRE AND I HAVE OUR LITTLE SECRET. I was fourteen during a summer in Normandy at the farm of our grandparents. We spent idle hours in the heat, idle hours listening to the buzzing of the flies, idle hours amusing each other with school gossip and fantasies of foreign places. One day in mid-afternoon, Claire found me reading beneath a large tree. "You must come with me."

I looked at her flushed face. "But why? Come where?"

She led me to the barn, cautioned me not to make a sound. We carefully climbed the rear ladder to the loft. Each time a board creaked, Claire froze, waited, then moved on again. I followed. The mystery of it held me now. Nothing so entertaining had happened since the day of our arrival. I was thoroughly amused and certain to be amused further. Claire finally led me to an opening in the floor of the loft. She peered over the edge at the barn below. Then she rolled her eyes and beckoned to me. I slid forward. I looked down. There upon a bed of hay some fifteen feet below us lay our mother and father.

I quiver at the memory. I sense the moment again, the smell of the barn, the heavy heat, the silence of the afternoon with every one in the house asleep. Mother and Father were not asleep. They lay upon the hay caught in each other's arms, kissing, whispering and kissing again, while above them Claire and I were afraid to breathe lest we giggle and reveal our presence.

The portent, of course, was of something more than mere kissing. Claire looked at me and smiled. She had knowledge of things. The look said: Now you shall see and thank me for it. I turned my eyes to the ground again, to the rustling and whispering. They were fondling each other now. Was Mother protesting? When they turned a bit, I could see Father's hand beneath her skirts. Then Mother's hand moved to the front of his trousers. She found what she wanted. She kissed him again. I was mesmerized by her hand, the play of her fingers, the squeezing. I could not see Father's hand. Mother's hip moved, squirmed. Father's hand had obviously found its goal.

Then Father mumbled, pulled away. He made Mother turn. At first she protested, pleaded, warned him of the danger. But Father insisted and in a moment she yielded. She turned and knelt upon the bed of hay. He raised her skirts to uncover the wide expanse of her bottom.

Broad and white. I remember the milk-white flesh of Mother's bottom, the two moons split by the crack. Father worked at his trousers to get them down to his knees, and for a moment Mother's hairy purse was completely visible at the joining of her thighs.

Then my eyes were drawn to the greater revelation. Father's magnificence had appeared. His rampant penis. His cock and balls surrounded by a dark forest of hair, the shaft pointing straight out and weaving as though in search of a target. He was quickly upon her, covering her bottom, mounting her from the rear, Mother groaning at the invasion of his organ. Father's hips moved, churned, pumped, and Mother brayed in happy response. Quite happy. I was old enough to know the meaning of that wailing sound.

The doing of it was brief. They were hurried by circumstance, by a fear of discovery. Father made a grunting noise as he emptied his ballocks. In which entrance? The question remains unanswered. At the end of it, they pulled apart from each other, quickly arranged their clothes and left the barn. Claire and I waited a few moments, and then we stole out of the place the way we had come. We hurried to the woods to fill our skirts with berries, to confirm our innocence if our absence had been noted.

The berries were picked, the skirts filled, the family united again at dinner. Grandfather and Grandmother, Father and Mother in complete decorum. Mother, as usual, cautioning her girls to avoid the sun.

* * *

And now again. This grate. This barred window into my sister's room. Am I now a prisoner? Edward stands near one of the chairs. He does not look at Claire. He holds a thin unlit cigar in his hand and he seems pensive. Claire is seated at her dressing table. She unpins her hair. She pouts. She shakes her head. "Do you want to, or shall I call Dobbin?"

Edward nods. He slips the cigar into one of the pockets of his waistcoat and he goes to Claire. She stands and he begins to work at the buttons and hooks of her dress.

Claire talks of someone called Cyril. One of Edward's friends? "He's a rogue, you know. He's an awful rogue. I told you that last Christmas, didn't I? I did tell you that."

"Yes, you did."

"One mustn't be deceived by people like that. I don't like to be deceived."

"I don't think he ever means any harm."

"That's nonsense, isn't it? Five thousand pounds' worth of nonsense."

She is in her chemise now, her body slender

beneath the white silk. Edward kneels to undo the buckles of her shoes. When he has her shoes off, he wants to bring her stockings down. But Claire pulls away and walks to the chaise.

He follows her at once. "Let me."

One after the other, he pulls the stockings down and off her feet. Claire makes a sound in her throat. She laughs. A bubbling laugh. "You're a nasty little sailor. I want it through my drawers."

Her thighs moved apart. Edward swoops. His face in her drawers. His mouth against the white silk. She fondles his head. She bends her head as she watches him.

And as I watch them both. My legs are unsteady. I stand upon a chair and my legs are unsteady. Edward at his dinner. The little sailor feeding at my sister's plate. Her thighs rocking. There is only silence now. An occasional murmur from Claire. My legs continually shaking. I watch the hand that strokes his head. Her narrowed eyes.

Then Edward pulls away. He rises. His fingers at his flies. His trousers unbuttoned. Claire is amused, smiling in her amusement. Edward's root appears. The dark pink of his root. Claire touches him, her fingers curling, her pink hand upon his pink root. Her slender fingers. She smiles. A soothing murmur. Yes, darling, yes. How randy you are. Her fingertips tickling. Edward quivers at the tickling of her fingertips. She strokes him, fingers curled, fingers tickling, stroking his root as he quivers before her. His eyes fixed upon it. His flushed face. Her fingers stroking. How swollen he is. The straining of his flesh. She murmurs again, calls him little sailor again.

I shall go mad. She has him panting. I shall go mad as I watch the doing of it. His eyes popping. The little sailor. Claire smiling. Her tickling fingers. I can feel the hot flesh. The heat rises to the grate and warms my face. What a marvelous vision. Edward in his chaos.

There is no ending. She drops her hand. She tells him to undress. Edward blubbers, his fingers working at his buttons. Claire moves to the bed, removes her drawers and then her chemise.

She waits. Edward is done, stripped, his body pale, his root in a frenzy. His balls jiggle as he moves. He climbs upon the bed, settles upon his back beside Claire. She snickers and turns. She straddles his pale body. She moves forward to fix her nest upon his mouth.

One must assume. When a cloud covers the moon, one must assume the moon is still there. Edward's face is covered. My sister's bottom and thighs obliterate his face. Her body rocks, a swaying movement as she presses against his mouth. Her neck is bent as she looks down. Is she murmuring? I think I hear the sound of it. A quiet chanting. Then she reaches behind her to fondle his root and balls, one arm behind her, her neck always bent, her body rocking, rocking. This pink metronome on my sister's bed. This pink arrangement in my sister's room.

Then the rocking stops. Claire shifting backward. Back to his essentials. She squirms over it, holding it, guiding it, then settling upon it as Edward makes a sound of contentment. His cock in her nest. My sister settles down upon her husband. Her bottom rolling. Now she moves again, up and down, up and down, riding Edward, riding in her saddle. Her back straight. The jiggling of her apple breasts. The curve of her rump as it rolls upon his pelvis. Edward's mouth is open. He mutters something but I can't make it out. Claire continues her ride. She smiles as she rides. Her voice cajoles him. The little sailor. His pale skin. The fierce passion shining in his face. His cock in her nest. His cock inside her cove. My sister's body rising and falling as she rides in her saddle. Oh, the sweetness of it. My face flushed in the heat of it. Edward growning now. Claire's amusement. Claire smiling as he spends.

* * *

Claire has an enduring enjoyment of propitious moments. There are four of us at a small dinner party: Claire and Edward, myself and a Mr. Walter Bramsby. We sit enthroned in our misconstructions, our small amusements. Our urgencies. I have the feel of it. I know the outcome. One must trust one's intuition. Walter Bramsby dabbles in the casual sarcasm enjoyed by Claire. Edward laughs. He drinks his wine. "Oh, that's capital."

"That's lovely."

"Yes, indeed."

"We mustn't be harsh now."

Our clothes are in fashion. I have powdered my shoulders this evening because Claire has insisted upon it. Edward is so charming. He shines at parties like this. His eyes have a shine of perfect comfort.

Walter Bramsby is clean shaven. I don't know if I find his face appealing. I think he might be more impressive with whiskers. His eyes are always upon me. His eyes upon my powdered shoulders. And why not? I think my shoulders are more easily looked at than Claire's. Darling girl, you're being horrid again. Completed horrid at another of Claire's banal dinners.

In the drawing-room, Edward and Walter light their cigars as Claire and I sip our sherry. Walter's eyes are upon me again. My shoulders. My bosom. His admiration is amusing. All women are fond of the eyes of men. We have our recognitions. We have our devices. It is not easy to obey one's will. Claire teases me. She calls attention to my hesitations. What does one see in the eyes? Does he have strong hands? I do like strong hands in a man. Oh yes, he will call. And Claire smiles as she thinks it. I hide my annoyance in my sherry glass. I have the image of them, the fervent couplings upon Claire's bed. I think the sherry is much too sweet. Edward keeps one hand behind his back and looks as pretentious as ever. I remember how he turned pink as Claire handled his root. His pink cheeks. They shut themselves up in that room, shut themselves away from the world.

After Walter Bramsby leaves, Claire coaxes me to say what I think. I detest the amusement in her eyes. She urges me. She smiles. "You must tell, darling." Her fingers fluttering at me. Edward agrees. "You need someone dependable." Again I have the images of them in Claire's room. Claire on the chaise with Edward's face at her copse. Do I want a suitor? Do I want Walter Bramsby to call upon me? Then one of the maids is in the room and I refuse to say anything. Edward sends the maid Perkin out. Claire talks of finding another maid, one more girl in the house. She teases Edward, asks if he agrees. Edward's eyes are distant. Claire turns to me and smiles. "You will be pleasant to Walter, won't you, darling?"

The clock strikes twelve and Claire begins again. I must gather myself together. I must make a life. I must avoid the pangs of melancholy. I need distraction. If Walter calls upon me, I should see him. "He has a fine voice when he sings."

* * *

And the grate again. My eyes are burning at the

grate. Claire again mounted on his face. Her night-dress gathered at her waist. Edward extended upon her bed in his dressing-room and Claire queening him with her bottom. She faces his feet this time. Her thighs glow in the yellow light of the electric lamp. How she queens him. His mistress. She ought to be wriggling madly. Edward's face burried by my sister's rump. When I first met him, he seemed so cavalier. I remember he was dressed in white, with a white boater and a white suit and immaculate white shoes. I remember the shoes best of all. I thought any man with shoes like that had to be of superior constitution. Then after Claire's betrothal I was in a desperate jealousy. Claire and her friends whispering to each other. Mother's glazed eyes. Mother always insisted we behave with dignity. Dignity in public and dignity in solitude. But of course there wasn't much dignity in that barn at the grange, was there? Her bottom turned up to Father's probing.

Claire is laughing now. "The other way, Teddy."

She dismounts, climbs off his face and turns. She kneels upon the bed, her night-dress still gathered at her waist, her bottom turned up like a rising moon.

Edward moves behind her, behind the moon, behind the ivory expanse. He hesitates. A mere moment. Then he drops to bury his face against her bottom.

Claire wriggles. A mewling sound. Her bottom against his face in her amusement.

Edward pays his homage. He nuzzles. He presses. I can see his nose between the globes. His mouth has vanished. To which aperture? In her rose-hole? I suppose she demands both. I turn to stone in my envy. The male tongue in the most secret place. How ridiculous we are. We want the probing, be it root or finger or tongue. And the loving admiration.

Obeisance. Only once with John and then I had too much wine to keep him there. But of course he wouldn't stay. Edward, perhaps, but not John.

How she rules him. His devotions. His tongue certainly in the quick of her bottom now. As she wriggles.

Then he's gone. He groans and turns on his back once more. Once again Claire mounts his face. Now she exposes his root, his swollen penis. She strokes him. She kneels over him, half-bent, her eyes fixed upon her doing, her fingers curled as she strokes him. Edward squirms. He touches one of her thighs. An appeal? Her hand continues to fondle him. To milk him. She coos at him, cajoles him. Her slender fingers milking his root. "All right, Teddy." The hand goes up and down with increased vigor. My sister's hand. Upon her husband's root. The ending foretold, but of course I shall watch it. I think tomorrow I shall walk in one of the parks with a parasol. I shall meet other women like myself. Do they have sisters like Claire? Now suddenly Edward makes a bleating sound and Claire's hand responds with a burst of fervor. Her fingers curled and squeezing. The crisis. He spouts. Again. Again. He calls out as she continues. She laughs. She pulls at his root with her hand. She bends over his face and kisses his lips.

Chapter Four

CLAIRE HAS GONE OFF TO MITCHAM to a meeting of the Society for Homeless Pets, while Edward and I do a promenade in Holland Park. We pretend. I hold Edward's arm and we pretend we are husband and wife. There is music somewhere, a band playing, the sound of voices. Edward pats my hand. Does he pretend with me? Does he have secret thoughts? Does he have hot and turbulent feelings? I want to know the surging in him. In Claire's absence. I want to know it. Or perhaps he thinks of nothing but his collection of shells and his tobacco and the disposition of his mother's house in Kensington. Men can be so trivial. They must be pointed to it like a hunting dog in training. They must be shown the way. I don't have a grudge against the world. I will not be unhappy. I don't like the idea of it. Darling, it's the jealousy that disturbs you. He must think of something. Edward is certainly not preoccupied with love and religion. So quiet this morning. His dignity. I must allow him to be himself. I have not watched in more than a week. He does not visit her room. No more mumblings in the dim light. Ellen Terry covers the grate and behind Ellen Terry the ghosts are silent. Here is one room and there another. I lie awake in my bed imagining a shuffling sound in the corridor. I lie awake with my odds and ends, irrelevant recollections of all sorts of little things. I would like to go dancing. I imagine myself dancing.

And these people we pass, these couples that walk in the park like ourselves, do they take me for Edward's wife? That young man, the girl upon his arm with inquisitive eyes. They ought to be riding together in a wood somewhere. Perhaps it was done yesterday. Laughing in a wood. The halting conversation. There is nothing as silly as an Englishman alone with a woman he wants. This fellow is thinking of the horses, of the stable, of India, of the presence or absence of the Crown in the Red Sea, anything to avoid thinking of the obvious, while beside him the girl quavers as she waits for an indication of something, of anything at all. Finally the moment in the wood arrives and she pants for pleasure. They kiss. She presses against him. He pulls back, begs her pardon, then kisses her again. Oh, I can see it. In another moment he nods at the horses and suggests they ought to return to the stable.

Edward pats my hand again. "Are you tired?"

"No, not at all."

"I do like walking with you like this."

"Is that a flower-bed?"

"Where?"

"Over there, at the edge of those trees."

"Yes, I suppose so."

"Let's have a look at it, shall we?"

Yes, we shall. I pull at his hand. I laugh as I make him hurry. Then I drop his hand and run. It's madness. I'm sure a thousand eyes are watching us. They think us lovers. And what does Edward think? He smiles as he comes up to me. I'm rather out of breath. I like it. I like the feeling. I take his hand again. How odd it is to hold the hand of my sister's husband. Does he find me beautiful? Do I have the power to charm him? How taciturn he is. I shall crumble his reticence. I feel the working of it, second by second. Heaven knows I want it. I say something silly and he smiles. In another moment he laughs. Men are so easily turned. I'm sure at breakfast this morning he had no thought in his head of holding my hand in the park. How amusing he is, at times so dull, at other times a hint of something in his eyes. I do like his smile. Is it important to like the way a man smiles? How strange it is to think of Edward apart from Claire.

At the flower-bed we stand side by side. Edward turns, presses against me, then suddenly mumbles an apology. I see a glint of metal in the distance, a motor car passing in the road. Are we watched? I don't think so. I see no passers-by. Edward leans to me again and this time he kisses me. First my cheek and then my lips. His hand upon my arm. His male hand. I look beyond the flower-bed again, but there is nothing to be seen. I quiver as he kisses me again. Shall I go to Oxford Street tomorrow? Shall I visit Atkinson's scent shop? Edward presses his lips against my own.

* * *

In the evening I sit with Walter Bramsby in a theater box. I think he's a mere boy. In the cab he talked of nothing but his business affairs. Then in the lobby of the theater his face was flushed as he gazed at my shoulders. His manners are so impeccable. I'm sure if he were French he'd manage the most correct little bow. He's a man incapable of an outrage, no matter if the outrage would save his life. We shall go on, we shall go on. I shall suffer these people around me, this theater crowded with Walter Bramsbys. I have the memory of Edward's kiss upon my lips. His apologies. He thinks himself so insolent. I ought to be with Edward now and not with Walter Bramsby. Walter is too awful. Walter is an intolerable ass. His business affairs, His society. The bowler hat he wears in the City. Yes, very eager. I wonder what sort of lover he is. I wonder concerning his attachments. His mother's blandishments. It's always the mother that produces the lover. Is he frightfully clever? I can't imagine it. Perhaps if he's cajoled.

They must be given things. They have their inducements. Tomorrow I shall have breakfast in bed and avoid any difficulty with Edward at the table. I shall breakfast in bed and think of myself as a duchess, a woman descended from one of the Henrys. I shall imagine myself in Chatsworth rather than Kensington. I feel such lethargy. This play. The voices emanating from the stage.

Then Walter takes my hand in his. I feel the warmth of his palm. How amusing it is. Is it the play, or thoughts of his mother, or an indication of sublime passion? Does he want me? Does he imagine us in a life together? His life with a Kensington widow? I think he doubts his own taste in things. I feel the softness in his hand, the idle years in London drawing-rooms. In a week he'll find some reason to offer me an expensive present. A pompous little present from an impossibly pompous man.

Darling, don't be awful. You mustn't be awful. I pull my hand away. Does it make him sad? I slide my hand over the cloth of his trousers. Now the moment of sadness is gone and he quivers. Shock and disbelief. Oh, you poor little boy. My fingers walking in his lap. I would work at his buttons, but I'm afraid poor Walter will faint. I want to feel the weight of his balls. They think it's the root we want, but of course it's the stones that command attention. John's plumpness in my hand. Always impressive without clothes. His nakedness. And Walter's nakedness. I imagine Walter naked. His white skin. Now I find him. My hand upon his part. His member. My fingers closing.

He whispers to me. Frantic whispering. "Julie, darling . . ."

"Bring it out."

"Good Lord, that's impossible."

But he does the impossible. His fingers fumbling

at his buttons. In a moment I have his huge thing in my hand. Stiff. Throbbing. More substantial than I expected. Oh yes indeed. Here in a box at the Criterion. Walter Bramsby's cock in my hand. His lengthening. His amorous extension. There is nothing as marvelous as the feel of it under one's fingers. The muscular jerking. How helpless he is. I have an inclination to laugh. I long to see his face clearly in the light. Now the pomposity is gone, the talk of business affairs, the comic sniffing.

He's well-formed. Indeed perfectly formed. The cowl easily down, the knob full and firm. He reminds me very much of John. Quite full in the bulb. Oh yes. Pity I can't have his cods in my hand. Hold them and confront the procreation of the race. Instead my fingers have the wicked serpent. Throbbing beneath my fingers. Walter Bramsby throbbing. How solemn he is. His eyes fixed upon the stage below, the actors, the scene, as I stroke his throbbing with my fingers. His face shows nothing that I can see. He's never been married. He thinks he wants to marry me. Or did think so when we entered the theater. And now that my hand holds his hot root, does he forgive my widowhood? So much force beneath my fingers. One wants to forget the man and adore the instrument.

I rub the stalwart soldier, amused at the eyes that occasionally gaze at us from the boxes across the stalls. They can't imagine that Walter's trousers are unbuttoned and his affair in my hand. This impressive instrument he has. He's pensive now. He thinks I'm a woman without scruples. He does not understand my intention. He quakes in my hand, but he does not understand my intention. He does not understand the talk of my fingers. Mr. Bramsby in a bout of persistent sang-froid. Stiff and hot. I clasp the heat of it. The fierce erectness of him. I would have more light to see the full view of it. What a state. He whispers again. "My darling! You must not." Well, yes I must. I must continue the operation. My hand filled, stroking, cajoling. His throbbing in my hand. The tip is leaking now and my fingers are bedewed with it. I would inspect it. The weeping. Walter Bramsby in my possession. So large. One can't imagine actually receiving it.

Then a sudden movement. Walter's voice, his desperation. His limb jerking beneath my fingers, throbbing in his desperation. His utmost extent. Another muted groan as he feels his pleasure. The spasm beneath my fingers. Hissing at me. "You drive me mad!" Pity I can't see the tip. With a large one like this. The finish now. My fingers working. He groans again at the final moment. His body jerking in his chair as he spends. His sweet sperm spouting out of his balls. An exquisite flood of it. Jetting out to splatter against the velvet of the balustrade.

Down below on the stage, someone laughs. Walter slumps in his chair. My fingers curl and squeeze, squeeze again, until finally Walter comes to his senses and offers me his handkerchief.

* * *

Edward mutters at me when he next finds me alone in the drawing-room. Something about a ball in Eaton Square. An invitation. Claire has no interest, but she would have us go. "A dance will do you good," Edward says. "I shall take you myself." It's not clever of him. It's much too dangerous. He sees my reticence. "I hope nothing is wrong."

I've come to a decision about Edward. I will have him. I shall not be satisfied until the doing of it.

He holds my hand. He kisses me. My lips. His flushed face. He's dreadfully excited. I glance down at the front of his trousers. I regard his excitement. The memory of Walter Bramsby in my hand is still fresh. Do I dare? Do I possess the audacity?

"Is Claire at home?"

"She's gone to Guy's Hospital."

"Whatever for?"

"I don't know. I think to comfort someone."

I touch the front of his trousers. "And you remain here to comfort me."

He closes his eyes. "It's not possible."

"You kissed me before."

"Yes, I suppose I did."

"Then it's possible, isn't it?"

His buttons come undone. His root appears. I coax him a bit and his balls come out. Lovely firm testicles. I examine Edward. I explore my sister's husband. His pride.

Yesterday Claire annoyed me with a relentless chattering about her friends at Croydon. I don't care about her friends at Croydon. Now Edward's penis twitches in my hand. This is not Croydon, this is Kensington. I feel lazy. How lovely it is to have an idle afternoon with Claire's husband. His endowments. He waits for my ministrations. I have the power of knowing it now. The feel of his flesh beneath my fingers. Will the door open? We stand in the bright morning sun, and if one of the maids should enter she will see everything.

Edward shudders. "We ought to go somewhere else."

"We oughtn't to be doing this at all. You're my sister's husband."

"I do know that."

"What do you want?"

"Want?"

"What do you want with me?"

"I don't know."

What does he think of women? The fairer sex. What logical faculties does he bring to bear upon the difference? Men have thoughts of Empire, but not much thought for the origins of things. His ramrod being. He's quite robust. Without his family's money, he might be somewhere in the territories. In the Foreign Service perhaps. Edward would be an excellent representative of English complacency. He says this is impossible but he stands imprisoned by my hand. How little one knows people. Edward's randy cock. He seems unsteady upon his feet. He ought to be sitting but I want him to stand. I want his mind upon my fingers. One must seek out the important things in people. The odd affinities. All these people I've never spoken to, never known. One must believe in the possibilities. One must have no illusions. One must depend only upon evidence. Good Lord, how warm he is! He mumbles something, but I ignore it. I have no interest in anything except what he exposes to me. His balls in my hand. His thick root. Thicker than Walter but not as long. One catalogues them for an empty moment. That fellow in Bloomsbury shortly after John and I were married. His ranting about our detestable social system and so forth while I brought him off in a brandy glass. Giggling as he spouted in a brandy glass. Walter two days ago and Edward today. Darling, it's too much. All this playing about with masculine tumescence. My sister's husband. His wife is my sister. The way he pleasures her in her bedroom. Her face. What she feels in her face.

"Kiss me, Edward."

"Come to my room."

"Now?"

"Yes, now."

"No, I don't think so. Kiss me here."

He kisses me as I continue holding his root in my

hand. His lips are warm. He touches my bosom. His fingers at the buttons. Yes, why not? I bare my breasts, hold them in my hands. "Kiss them."

His lips upon my breasts. His lips enclosing a nipple. How delicious. How nice. The sensation is exquisite. I run my fingers around his neck. His hand holds my breast as he kisses it. The other hand slides around to squeeze my bottom. He pulls at me with his lips as I grip his testicles. He mumbles about his room again. No, I won't have it. My legs are weak but I won't have it. I want him to suck my breasts in Claire's drawing-room. I want an intimate understanding of things. That fellow in the Times prattling about natural causes. What do they understand of natural causes? What does Edward understand? I'm sure he had Claire before they were married. And other French girls. Englishmen adore French girls. They say the French girl knows how to bring the passion out of a man. Out of an Englishman. One brings the passion out of an Englishman with fingers and lips. How harmless he is. He will suck at my breasts forever if I don't stop it. He wants to touch other places but he lacks the will. He wants the favors only lovers are permitted. My sister's husband. His red cheeks. His lips pulling at my nipples. My bonbons.

Finally I pull away. The danger is too great. His eyes are pleading.

Chapter Five

"YOU'RE AN EXQUISITE WOMAN."

"It's Claire who's your wife."

"Come to my room."

"Your room? No, I don't want your room."

He falls upon me again. On his knees. He holds my foot and kisses it, a lovely kiss, his tongue fluttering. His agitation is amusing. What a delight he is. His lips are sensual. Another kiss. The other foot. Silence now in the room as Edward is at my feet. Then he looks up at me, his hand stroking, his eyes feverish.

"Do you want to drive me mad?"

"Don't be silly."

"I think you want to drive me mad."

I pull my foot away. I wonder what he was like before they married. He seems so weak with Claire, as if he wanted it. But he maintains a degree of dignity. Even upon his knees, he maintains a degree of dignity. Does he have a stand? He waits for me. I amuse myself in the waiting. How absurd it is. How ordinary. We must have something better than this. That awful fellow from Zurich who kissed my feet and then fell over dead drunk on the rug.

Now Edward is at my legs again, his hands pushing at my dress, his hands upon my calves, his murmuring. He wants the central spot, darling. He's like a puppy-dog. One must have tenderness for the passion of the male. Completely aroused. I ought to make an effort at modesty. My legs are exposed, my knees, my garters. Edward is at my body. He presses himself upon the fortress. His face pushing at my thighs. One thinks of the delicious prospect. His lips quivering against my thighs. My dress pulled up. My thighs so wantonly exposed. He mumbles again. Is he really so intoxicated? Now he removes a shoe. Then the other. Then he wants my stockings off. His fingers tickling my feet. His greedy eyes upon my legs. How delightful it is. This lechery that he shows in his face, this abandoned devotion to the senses. I want to see him naked. I want to look at his cock and balls. How silly he looks as he kisses my knees. You're a wanton, darling. You revel in your wantonness. How lovely it is. His mouth. Does he understand the meaning of it? I wonder if Claire is amused when he kisses her legs. His back bent. This homage they pay to the woman. I won't go upstairs with him yet. Certainly not yet. I must have something here in the drawing-room. Something to remember. One always needs something to remember.

He looks at my face now. "Let me see it."

"See what?"

"Julie, please . . ."

The puppy-dog begging. "Darling, you mustn't."

"Yes, I must."

He goes on, his fingers pulling at my drawers, at the bows that hold them. My drawers come down. I must raise my hips. An accomplice. My dress falls again to hide my belly. He succeeds in slipping my drawers off my feet. He returns to my thighs again, pushing at my dress to gradually expose what he wants.

I show reluctance. One must always show reluctance. But then my belly is uncovered. My nest. Edward's eyes are upon me, his hands upon my body. I sigh. I pretend to be reconciled to it. His gaze. How much force and power it has. His eyes show an intense gratification. His senses overwhelmed as he contemplates the realities. His face so close to the realities. I have the pleasure of it. I like to be looked at. I like the close perusal of my little garden. I like the pleasure in their eyes. How intoxicating it is to be looked at like this. He whispers at me. He splutters. His face. His lips. The tickling sensation of his breath. He reveals himself. His salacious temperament. I want to see him. His instrument. The lewdness of him naked. Seduced by the Devil, darling. You want the sensation of having your sister's husband. Yes I do. Well, I already have him in a sense. His face at my copse. Just looking. The anticipation in his eyes. What does he see? The intrigue of the feminine flower? How silly they are sometimes. One thinks of the passion. One imagines the pleasures. Claire's husband. Well, we've already gone too far to draw back. Is he pleased? The way they well with lust. We ought to be wary of the door. One of the maids might come in. Or both maids at once. Edward upon his knees in front of me, his face between my thighs, his mouth almost upon me, his nose sniffing at me. Does he have a taste for sweets? Shall I grant the favor of it? How wicked it is. His eyes burning upon my slit. Madamoiselle? His amorous fancies. Shall I confess the truth? Shall I tell him how much I adore displaying myself? Shall I tell him how much I adore what he is about to do? I want to excite him. I want his lust. I want his confirmation. Yes, I suppose that's what it is. His confirmation. One gets confirmed each time it's done. The kiss. The intimate kissing. Now, Edward, now. Yes, darling, you have him now. His breath. He nuzzles first. Delay. Exquisite dalliance. Finally I groan and pull at his head. The darling man. His mouth. The pleasure of it. I groan. My head back. My hands upon his temples. I squirm upon the cushion. His tongue in my furrow. Up and down. Over and over again. His head moving. How he kisses it. His lips. The tickling of his breath. What an agony of delight it is. His tongue in the wet. Yes,

Edward. In the quick of it. Does Claire feel the same? Do sisters feel the same? The way she laughs. He pushes at me, his mouth pushing, his lips pushing. My legs upon his back. His face against my nest. I don't want to groan. I don't want him to hear that. I must pretend a degree of coolness. A small degree. He must not know the disturbance he causes. His face down there. His nose. Sometimes when he looks at me, his interest is so prominent. It's a wonder Claire hasn't guessed it. I must not cry out. Silly girl, you must not cry out. He won't understand it if you cry out. People never do understand it. And the servants. We must leave this room. I want to leave this room but I will not release him. I will not release his mouth. And the pleasure to come. His wet kiss. How lovely it is. His delight is so intense. The way he delights in it. His lips so fervent. The sweet sucking. Now he has the taste and smell of me. His wife's sister. The sound of it. How impatient he is. It's marvelous to have it done with such vigor. Go on, darling. Be as nice as you can. Find whatever you want. I do like it. Oh Lord, I do like it.

* * *

In my bedroom now. I refused his room. I want him here, the doing of it on my bedroom. His trousers unbuttoned. His organ in my hand. The exhibition. The lust in his eyes. How obscene it is. The pink instrument. He murmurs. My fingers linger. The moment voluptuous, trembling with a portent of pleasure. My mind is in a whirl. Now that I have him in my hand. The excitement of holding him. Claire's husband. His swollen limb. The lingering feel of his efforts in the drawing-room. My curled fingers upon his vigor as he kisses me. His determination throbbing beneath my fingers. I stroke him. He groans. I test his inclinations, his lust. Then he groans again as I sit upon the edge of the bed and bring him forward. His knob between my lips. I draw at the tip. His pego sucked. He shudders. I want his ballocks out. He groans as I lift his balls, tickle the big stones. His root stiff and swollen in my mouth. He mumbles something, shows his agitation, his fingers touching my cheek. Then I release him and rise, kiss his lips, slide my arms around his neck and kiss his lips again. My thighs pressed against his. His penis stiff against my belly. I look down at it. I play with it. Once again I sit on the edge of the bed and suck it. How fiercely erect he is. The heat of his flesh in my mouth. His huge thing. My fingers lifting his cods, his delicious balls. Slowly, darling. You don't want him spending now. Not will all his clothes on. You must enjoy the moment. You must have the full sweetness of it.

We undress. Edward in haste. His white body appears, his cock extended, flushed pink, his balls in a nest of brown hair. He helps me drop my clothes. Then I fall upon the bed and in a moment his lips are at me. My feet. He groans as he kisses my toes. He groans in his anguish. I recline backwards. Then I lift my head again to watch him kiss my belly. A private view of Edward in his passion. His excitement. He strokes my legs. His hand slides between my thighs to find my nest.

How easy it is to yield to it. The stroking. The kissing. The strangeness of it because this is Edward at my copse. Edward's fingers. One has one's obligations. We have our minor courtesies. I did not expect his passion. He has a certain quality in his manner, something admirable. He touches my breasts with his outstretched hand. We have such power over them. The female charm has such enormous power over their will. One would think they should resent it, and perhaps they do. Perhaps tomorrow he will hate me. But now I have his delight. I have him naked upon my bed. My bedroom. The room next to Claire's. His hands clasped around my bottom. His body is half-twisted to the side and I can see just the tip of his root, the pink knob of it. Moist and pink. Oh yes, the anticipation now. He kisses me again. Our lips joined. His fingers in my sex to indicate his intention.

"I must have you."

"We'll be sorry for this."

"You mustn't think of Claire."

"But I do think of Claire. She happens to be my sister and I do think of her."

"I won't let her come between us."

He makes me kneel. Desperation in his face now, his cheeks flushed in his desperation. He will not be put off. I kneel upon the bed and in a moment his knees are between my thighs. A soft pillow cushions my head. My breasts droop down as I bend before him. He murmurs as he strokes me with his fingers. Then he pushes at me. His organ pushing at my sex. How potent he is. His rammer pushing in, sliding inside. The broad head in the wet opening. I adore the first stretching during the entrance. He moves in, fills my channel. The first thrust. A sound in his throat. My slit penetrated. I am completely taken. His cock full in. His balls pushing against my clitoris. One has all of a life, a whole life. Some things repeated and diminished in the repetition. But not this. The fundamentals remain undebauched. The other day in the park, a woman shouted as she championed the down-trodden. No more than a dozen steps behind her, a shop window announced the new price of Swiss chocolate. And not far beyond that, the House of Commons debated the latest incident in Morocco. None of it really matters, does it? One hesitates to believe it matters. We are such little creatures. Edward's root is thrusting now, continually sliding. My sex vanquished. His hands upon my hips. He bears forward. He plumbs my depths. I groan now. I groan at the fierce thrusting. Groaning and gasping. The way he grips me round the haunches. Quickly now. Quick and short. Oh yes. Spend, darling. Spend in the heat of it. Spend in the lovely heat of it. What a marvelous stroke he has. Vigor and will. The world turns around with vigor and will. His jetting now. He grunts like a boar. Pummels me. Pushes at me. Squeezes me as he empties himself.

* * *

So it is done. I lie here alone. Edward is gone. Claire has returned to the house. Am I happy? My mood is distracted. I'm bored. I touch my breasts. The fullness of my sex. I wonder what people would say. I wonder what people would look at. I think of his eyes when he looked at my nest. I'm tired of everything. Now that the business is done, I'm tired of it. Claire, after all, is his wife. Is she happy? One could take her for being happy. I touch myself. My sex. My clitoris. Oh darling, you can't. But why not? I want to cry. I feel no desire for anything. I hear sounds. I think I hear them talking. I have a feeling of rancor. I want nothing. Shall I have a holiday? All the whisperings are superfluous. All the murmurings. One must do everything. One must always do something quite different. I imagine him again. His mouth at me. His tongue. Edward's tongue. Yes, I did like that. His eyes. Now we know so much more of each other. In one day everything has changed. Was it necessary, darling? Yes, I do think it was. I hope it was. The clouds are gone now. Ellen Terry still stares at the heavens but the clouds are gone now. Is she satisfied? Does Edward understand it? Tomorrow I shall walk in the rain as I think of it. The strangeness of it. Now I have the fear that Claire will discover it. Would Claire understand it? No one would care if she did. She might laugh. She might say how foolish I am. She always says how foolish I am. She says my life has always been foolish. She says I was foolish to marry John. She says I'm unable to control my feelings. And Edward? He reeks with such indomitable egotism. His cods are so pink. One doesn't know a man until one has held his balls in one's hand. Next time I shall wear green silk drawers. Perhaps he wants me because I'm the younger one, the younger woman. Now we have something set down between us. A memory of frenzy. I was once a married woman, a wife. How curious it is to be something else again. How curious it is to once again know the sweetness of secrecy. Oh darling, you're a silly girl. You make so much out of a tawdry little poke in the afternoon. A few minutes of tongue-work in the drawing-room and a few minutes of pushing and pulling in the bedroom. No surprises, were there? Should I spill tears because there were no surprises? I am without the least shame. The way he licked me on the sofa. The feel of his nose against my clitoris. His cheeks. I thought of it from the first moment I kissed him. His face. His hand on my bottom. How extraordinary it is to have things progress so much according to prediction. We play with each other. Two children playing their little game. Two frivolous children. Claire is such a silly chatterbox, I suppose she deserves to be deceived by him. She reigns over him like a queen. I want to sleep. I want to be asleep. I don't want to think of it any more. His root. His mouth. My fingers in the quick. Tomorrow I shall stroll in the park and think of it again. The way he looked at me. The way he had his look at me. His curving over me. How awful it will be if he's not discreet. Don't pretend now. You must go on. I don't like distractions. I don't like the noise, the motor cars in the road. I don't like to be distracted when I do it. I'm fidgeting again. I shall have a look at my diamonds. No, you will not have a look at your diamonds, you will finish it. You poor wretch, you will finish it. Aren't you tempted to finish it? How absurd it is to be doing it here. So soon after. So wet again with the memory of it. His passion. The silence in the drawing-room as he licked me. My happiness. Julie is happy. I'm happy as a duck in a pond. What a happy little darling I am.

Chapter Six

WE HAVE AN EVENING AT THE COSMO CLUB. Claire giggling as we enter. Walter Bramsby looks distinguished. An evening jaunt. A powdered flunkey in the vestibule. Then we walk down. Shall we sup on the balcony? Claire would like a table on the main floor. She says the people in the balcony are all from South Kensington. On the main floor we settle at a table and Edward orders champagne. Couples crowding the dance floor. Bare backs and throbbing violins. Barristers, bankers, doctors, here and there a duchess from Belgravia. My bosom is almost bared. I feel the eyes of the men. The eyes of Edward and Walter. The eyes of the others. People in crowds are awful. Edward glances at me. Our secret. He sits opposite me and I can't avoid his eyes. Is he uneasy? I feel nothing. Not a shred of anxiety. Not a speck of guilt. I suppose I ought to feel guilty, but I don't. One can't contrive it when it doesn't exist. I am arrogant in the absence of guilt. I suppose I shall be punished for it. I suppose I shall suffer misery for it. Edward yearns for me. He says so. He says he dislikes the hours without me. The days and evenings. We can rarely touch each other in the evening. And during the day I have Walter's doting. His letters. His carriage is always waiting. He wants to force my love. I don't love him. I will not tell him that I love him. I suppose Claire would tell him something. She despises hesitations. She would commit the gravest sin rather than dawdle in a hesitation. She smiles at me now. She feels very much at ease in places like this. Walter seems to be writhing in discomfort. He's waiting to dance with me. He's jealous each time I laugh at something Edward says. He's too well brought up to push himself at me. I suppose he blushes each time he remembers that lark in his theater box.

Claire doesn't want to dance yet. She wants to look. All these smart people dancing the Boston. And the others not smart at all. The smiles of the women.

"I do like rhythm," Claire says.

"Talking nonsense."

"Bad style . . ."

"They respect nothing . . ."

"Look how she's clutching him."

"That woman's worse."

A feeble laugh from somewhere behind me. Walter's tie is white and his face is pale. Edward's cheeks are pink. Claire has shadows in the hollows of her cheekbones.

The music goes on, the dancing. What will things be like in six months? If only I could tell. I think Claire looks tired. Her eyes look bleak.

"That's just when I don't like them."

"It's a bit of a pose, isn't it?"

"I could sit and watch people all day long."

"It's not day, it's evening."

"Edward, don't be a bore. Why can't you be as charming as Walter?"

"There's something to be said for that."

"Look at that one."

"Substantial."

"She's enormous. Don't you think so, Julie? Don't you think that woman is enormous?"

Yes, the woman is enormous, a regal woman with voluptuous curves. A brocade gown and jewels at her throat. She dances with a man with a drooping moustache. One imagines them afterward in a bedroom in Belgravia. He tells her to open her legs properly. She has laughter in her eyes. Her fingers hold his root. She opens her white thighs to his gaze. He approves. A bubble of saliva forms at his lips. She holds the pose. She holds his affair. Then she rises. She turns with a swaying of her hips. Her eyes glitter with wickedness. She moans softly as he strokes her rump. Then her knees sag upon the bed. She kneels. She wriggles. His fingers tease her bottom-hole. He finds no rebellion. He pushes at her, he thrusts. She moans again, her tongue peeping. She moans and hangs her head as he corks her fundament.

I do like the dancing. The feet are curious, the spats and shoes with high heels, the buckles and buttons. Walter's eyes are upon my breasts again. I like his white gloves. I would have him again in a theater box. I would have his root beneath my fingers.

Another couple dances near our table. The woman laughing. I think of them together. His knob pushing at her slit. The tightness of her sex. His mouth twitching as he takes her. The rhythmic movement. Their feet sliding as they dance.

We dance at last. I dance with Walter. He gazes at my bosom. My shoulders are bare. His hair gleams under the light of the chandeliers. His hand presses against my back. Does he want me? His face is so vague. He says he thinks of me. He says I dispel his loneliness.

Is he truly lonely? He ought to have nothing to do with me. His tone is so earnest. He has no understanding of selfishness. I think that's his greatest fault. He smiles constantly. "I'm very fond of you, Julie." I think of his root. How shocked he was in that theater box. How easily devastated he is. I should like to expose him here. His masculine part dangling as we dance. He talks of dinner tomorrow. I don't want to promise anything. All these people around us. What does he think about? I gaze at his eyes, but I can never understand what he thinks. We glide past a group of women cackling at each other with their noses raised. Walter does dance decently. He has dreamy eyes as he follows the music. He wants romance. His lips are finely made. His mouth has a certain softness. Does he want the truth? No, he does not want the truth. He wants a life of fine sentiments.

When I dance with Edward, the mood is something else. We are here in peculiar circumstances. Claire now dances with Walter. I am in Edward's arms while my sister glides with the man who is my suitor. Edward and I glide with our secret. Our scandal. His face beams. One would think his features suffused with spiritual expression. He seems so happy to have me in his arms again. Perhaps he's not used to it. His eyes devour me. "I've been thinking of you all evening."

"Indecent thoughts, I suppose."

"I should think so. I want to make love to you."

"Darling, not here."

"When?"

"I don't know when. I don't think we ought to."

"You can't mean that."

"But suppose I do."

"I won't have it."

The situation is evidently completely hopeless. We must compromise. We are under Claire's gaze. She smiles at me as we pass. I soothe Edward. At intervals I press against him. His mouth is wet. He whispers at me. He says he's grateful to have me in his arms again. He says he wants to kiss me. He whispers at me that he will put his lips everywhere. His passion is so fierce. I want to touch his root. I want to hold his balls. I want to feel his urgency. I want to feel his quivering.

* * *

"He does it constantly," Claire says.

"Does what constantly?"

She frowns. "Oh, you haven't been listening again."

Tea in the drawing room an hour after lunch. "Please tell me."

"I said Edward is always after the maids. Now it's the new one."

"But we do the same."

"That's quite different."

"I don't see how."

"And John?"

"Yes, of course."

"I don't like it when Edward does it."

"Darling, you can't be jealous of a maid."

"It's not jealousy. I don't know what it is, but it's not jealousy. Edward is so incorrigible. I wish he were more like Walter Bramsby."

"That's ridiculous."

"I think he adores you."

"Who does?"

"Walter, of course."

"Don't be silly."

"I can tell by the way he looks at you. I can always tell by the eyes."

"He's a puppy."

"But sweet."

"Yes, that too."

"Will you marry him?"

"I don't think so."

"You do look lovely together. You look made for each other. Do you think Edward and I look made for each other?"

"Yes, I've always thought that."

"Walter does love you."

"Oh, hardly at all. Or only in the smallest degree."

"I do want you to be happy. You know that, don't you? I do want you to be happy."

"I'm not unhappy now."

"I think you need a husband. Every woman needs a husband."

"That's too conventional."

She laughs. "Yes, I suppose it is. You were always the unconventional one, weren't you?"

"I did marry John."

"And you won't marry again?"

"I don't know."

Selby comes in. The new maid. Edward often talks to me about her. He says she has an exquisite bottom. He says her rose-hole is exquisitely tight.

* * *

Claire has a birthday party. The house is filled with guests. Claire beams with the pleasure of it. People are so easily pleased. I don't like society. I find these people hopeless and stupid. I hate the chatter. The long hours of a dull party to celebrate my sister's birthday. How tedious it is. The doings in the smoking room. The pretensions of the overdressed women as they snicker at some latest amusement. The pompous conversations of the men as they estimate each other's income. Claire has provided a sequence of juvenile entertainments for the guests. She loves her deevy parties. She is so charming. I mustn't sneer because she is so charming. I mustn't be malicious towards my own sister. It's not pleasant. One wants to be pleasant. One wants a perfect existence. One wants all the qualities of a heavenly life. These pink and blonde English faces. Not a puzzled face in the mob. They want to have their fun. The eyes glitter, the cheeks glitter, the jewels glitter. I am too stupid to like it. The only thing important here is to have thirty thousand a year and a fresh crop of servant girls at Christmas. One must always be with the right people. One must be with people well suited to one's inclinations. I do think of the future but I see nothing. Am I unwilling? I have images of myself and Edward upon my bed. And images of Claire and Edward upon her bed. I feel an immense jealousy. Claire is jealous of the maids and I am jealous of Claire. Her gown is exquisite. Her eyes are lovely. Her complexion is perfect. She seems ravishing this evening. She floats like a bird. For whose benefit? For Edward's? I don't know. I don't know what she thinks. She always possesses someone. All the years of her life there was someone to be possessed. Every morning I am alone. I live in the world, but the world goes on without me. I watch them at night. Not always. He visits her room less often these days. On occasion she groans. One has the aspect of many things. My evenings with Ellen Terry. My turmoil afterward. The feeling of complete devastation. I ought to lose myself here in entertaining conversation. I ought to be coquettish. Walter Bramsby is in the house somewhere. Instead I think of the grate, I think of Claire and Edward laughing on her bed. You're grumbling, darling. You make the most awful connections. Now Claire takes me away to meet someone. Another unfamiliar face. A thin-lipped gentleman from Oxford murmuring that he once knew John. Sometimes I do miss John. If John were here, I should not have to talk to these people. Or is my impression a result of bitterness? The men are drinking too much. In a minute they'll be kissing the maids. How awful it is to be in a room filled with people when all the people are totally blind. Does Edward have other women besides the maids? Does he have a mistress in Portobello Road? Claire's face is so radiant. Is she mocking me? Is Claire mocking me?

Then Walter is at my side. He takes me away. He questions me. His curiosity. He shows the inevitable sweetness. His eyes pleading in his tormented face. His pleading eyes. He says he admires me. He says he hopes to be my companion. He says he hopes we shall find a spiritual union. His forehead is damp. His hand is damp upon my arm. He wishes to dance. What does one do with a perspiring suitor? I smile. I receive a grateful look in reply. Will he write me love letters? Then he says nothing. He seems detached as he looks around him. How absurd it is to be in his arms, to be dancing at Claire's birthday party with Walter Bramsby. How absurd it is that he has intimate memories of me. He thinks of the encounter in the theater box. Do I know what I want? I want a kiss. I want a sensation of pleasure. I want a feeling of ardor. Instead I have his damp hands. He looks at me again and now I have the longing in his eyes. My misfortune is a deflated balloon somewhere over the Channel. The London Ballooning Society expresses its sympathy to the widow of John Haversham. Walter Bramsby expresses his sympathy to the widow of John Haversham. How bored I am. I thought I would like the party, but I don't like it at all. Will Walter be offended if I tell him how bored I am? Perhaps he thinks me frivolous. Perhaps he thinks only a frivolous woman would fondle a man in a theater box. How stupid he is. I feel the impulse again. I want to hold his root. I want to feel his throbbing. Careful, darling, you'll make an awful scene. You must main tain self-control. You must make an effort of will.

You must uphold your dignity.

Later Edward takes me away to the library. He sees the tedium in my face. How considerate he is. He chuckles in his amusement. He says the people in the house are a silly lot. Claire's friends. Too many foreigners. Too much noise. "It might be better to have a moment of quiet. Claire won't mind. I have something new from Turkey. Do you like gold coins? I expect you've never seen any like these."

The library door is closed, and in a moment my eyes are confronted with the ancient coinage of Asia Minor. All his life Edward has collected things. How obstinate he is about his trivialities. He touches my arm. Is he certain Claire hasn't seen us? Men are so careless. Or perhaps he wishes to provoke a storm. He beams at me. He plays with his gold coins. His interests are so old-fashioned. Gold coins and Saracen daggers. Then he whispers at me that he wants to make love to me again. Shall we have an occasion? A twitch at the corner of his mouth. He breathes heavily. The lust in his eyes is absolute. I have my triumph. I glance at the front of his trousers. I see the firmness.

"I don't know when. Edward, it's impossible."

Dejection in his eyes. "You can't imagine . . ."

A sort of stupor comes over him. What does he want? Our situation is completely outlandish. He remains Claire's husband. He touches my arm. We shall be condemned by society. He leans close to me. He kisses me. His hand moves along my arm. His hand moves again and covers one of my breasts. I touch the front of his trousers. He quivers with excitement. I touch him again. My fingers trace the stiffness. My fingers work to undo his buttons. In a moment I have it. I have his root in my hand. His knob blushes. I push back his cowl to uncover the nut. I squeeze the tip. Edward groans. "My darling . . ." He stands in evening dress with his penis exposed. Long and hard. What mischief, darling. His root dangling. His face glows. His breath is warm upon my cheek. Claire's husband. Is there any suspicion? Edward murmurs in my ear. My hand closes upon his girth. He whispers at me. "You drive me mad!" How impatient he is. We both watch my hand. My fingers stroking, sliding the cowl back and forth over his angry knob. His face is flushed. He mumbles at me. How nice it is. His excitement in my hand. The pleasure in his throat. His handkerchief appears. "Good Lord!" He spends. I feel the twitching in his root as he spends. I finish the milking. Squeezing the flesh. His groaning as he finishes. His murmuring.

* * *

Walter shows me his house in Beauchamp Place. He talks of marriage. He says the essential thing is that we are spiritually alike. He says we shall manage beautifully. His illusions drip from his lips. How tempting it is. Shall I be a wife again? I am weary. "Walter, I don't think I can devote myself to you."

He nods. He says he admires my directness. He says he wants me to love him. He says he wants me to find myself. He says that after John's awful tragedy, I must regain my happiness. How blind he is. Does he think of my body?

"Let me beg you to consider . . ." He talks of possibilities. He talks of his intentions. His eyes are so sensitive. I am unwilling. I find it impossible to attempt anything. On the wall there is an engraving of Nelson at Trafalgar. Nelson on deck, gazing down at us, gazing down at the comical mess. I must have tolerant consideration. Walter says I must not act impulsively. He says we shall certainly enjoy a spiritual life together. He makes a vague gesture at his books. I have an impression of desperation. Then he moves to me. He kisses me. We cuddle against each other. He talks of marriage again. I think of uncomfortable crowding in a bed meant for one. How ridiculous it is to be courted. The intoxication in his eyes. Then he kisses me again and this time he presses against my body. His arms enfold me. He makes a mumbled pleading. He falls to his knees. His face presses against my legs. He pulls at my dress. I stroke his hair. I smile. I tell him I want to sit down. I must sit down. He crawls after me as I find a chair. On his knees. He rubs my thighs. I pull at my gown to expose my legs. He rubs my legs. He rubs the brown silk of my stockings. He kisses my knees. Subtle kisses upon my knees. Then the kissing is more fervent. His fingers above my stockings. A sound in his throat as he kisses the bare flesh of my thighs. The first time. His lips brushing across my skin. How amusing it is. I feel the tickling of his lips. I pull my gown further. My garters exposed. My nest exposed. His nose twitches. His face is flushed. Does he have my scent? Or is it the scent of my perfume stick? His lips are upon me. His face pressed against my source. Kissing in the quick. His lips against my nest. His nose pushes into me. His tongue pushes into me. I raise one leg to make the copse more available. He forages. He drinks from my tap. How sweet it is. You lack modesty, darling. I gaze down upon his head. He strokes my thighs with his hands as he sucks at my flower. His mouth absorbed. His tongue. I spend easily. My clitoris rubbed by his nose. His lips. My spending upon his lips.

* * *

Edward drives with me in St. James's Park.

"Will you marry him?"

"Do you want me to?"

"Certainly not."

"Then I won't."

He sighs. His eyes are puzzled. He talks about Claire. He asks about my doings in London. Am I comfortable in the house? He shows concern for my tranquility. He says we have our sympathies. He says he thinks of me often. He says he thinks of me often when he is with Claire. He knows nothing of the grate. He knows nothing of Ellen Terry. He has no idea how much I've seen. Their privacies. In the evening he drinks too much. I caution him. I speak of complications. He smiles. He says it's of no importance. He says our discovery of each other is important. How confident he is. Has Claire guessed? She always shows such innocence. She displays such benign approval whenever Edward and I speak to each other. Edward says his gravest sin is a lack of impatience. He talks of his club. His talks of his irritations with his acquaintances. He holds my hand. We've had no touching since the evening of Claire's birthday party. Is he randy? I have a yearning to tickle him. He kisses me. "I suppose you think . . ." He speaks of married life. He says my sister is no longer passionate. One feels so awkward in the midst of false confessions. I have seen them. I have seen Claire's enjoyment. And his own. Poor Edward has no idea I have seen them. He presses my hand. I do know what he wants. He wants me to do it again. What I did in the library the evening of Claire's party. I unbuttoned his flies. He mutters. He says he finds me bewitching. He says he is bewitched by the dexterity of my fingers. His penis is quite stiff, the cowl retracted. I tickle the shaft, the swollen knob. He kisses me. Is there any danger we'll be seen? Edward seems not to care. He chuckles as I explore further. I bring his ballocks out, his full stones. His cods are now bulging out of his flies. His virility is impressive. I tell him we must get home soon. I fondle his root. My hand stroking. "I don't want it on my dress." His handkerchief again. I stroke and tickle his hot flesh. His chest heaves. He makes a noise in his throat as he breathes. His knob is so polished. Does Claire do this? Does she milk him when she has the inclination for it? Her fingernails are so carefully manicured. What is he thinking of? His root throbs in my hand. Rose pink. The knob is a darker color, the tip glistening. More quickly now. His head back. A spurt. A groan. I cover the point with his handkerchief. Milk him quickly. Milk him into his handkerchief. His essence. No sound except his groaning and the clapping of the horses' hooves. The carriage rolling through the quiet park.

Chapter Seven

"YOU CAN'T AVOID ME," Edward says. "You've been avoiding me for days."

"It's not true."

"Yes it is."

"You're being preposterous."

"Julie, you mustn't . . ."

His face is flushed. It's true, of course. I have been avoiding him, refusing his whispers, refusing his touches whenever Claire's attention is elsewhere, whenever Claire is out of the house. Now he puffs at me. I tease him. I smile. I pull away when he touches my arm. I tell him it's too dangerous. I warn him of the eyes of the servants. The maids glide silently back and forth as we stand in the drawing-room. The new girl has ash blonde hair and blue eyes. Her name is Selby. She stares at us. Edward orders her out and the girl blushes as she leaves. He puts his hand upon my arm again. I have the memories of him. The frenzied moments as he poked me in my room. Is Claire suspicious? A breeze arrives through the open window to cool my throat. Then Perkin brings the tea. Edward tells her he will serve it himself. When the maid leaves, he pleads again. I mustn't avoid him. He can't bear it. He thinks of me constantly. He goes on and on.

One thrills to the adventure of it. This new aspect of Claire's house. Does Edward see the humor in it? Is he curious about the outcome? He looks unhappy. He looks to be in the midst of enormous suffering. He wants to be at me again. At least a display. The way I showed myself to him. Darling, you ought to blush for it. But I don't blush. His eyes were so lustful as he looked at my sex. One always wants that. I am not to be reproached for it. Now he lifts teacup in a trembling hand. Then he puts cup and saucer down and he makes me do the same. He takes me in his arms. A kiss. His lips upon mine. His arms about my waist. I can't refuse him. Claire is out and he will not be refused. His mouth is warm. His appetite suffuses his face with a pink glow. Well, how far can it go? Shall we have an idyll under Claire's nose? He whispers at me, tells me how often he thinks of me. His hands constantly move, constantly searching out my body beneath my clothes. Surely one of the maids will see us. Our illicit pleasures. He kisses me again and says he adores me. Yes, the parlormaids will see us. He doesn't care. He's a man favored by fate. Yesterday at dinner he looked at me with such lechery in his eyes, but Claire was oblivious. Now my attention wanders as he kisses my throat. I hear the slow ticking of the small gilt clock on the mantel. The sun falls, the shadows lengthen. I think Claire ought to have that immense sideboard put elsewhere. It looks so ugly here in the drawing-room. It ought to be in the dining-room. Behind Edward. How pompous he is when he advances a toast at the head of the table.

* * *

The new girl is completely docile. She kneels as she bathes my feet. Her blonde curls tremble. A girl with ivory skin and blonde curls and empty blue eyes. She blushes at my nakedness. She washes each foot as she blushes. Then I push at her, my foot pushing at her bosom. I amuse myself with a maid. Her eyes are upon my nest. When the wash is finished, she looks at my nest again.

"I want you undressed."

"Miss?"

"Undressed. Stand up and undress."

She quivers as she stands. Her maid's clothes fall away, her cotton underclothes. Her body is as white as her face, a pale white with here and there a slight flush of pink. I lie upon the bed. I order her to lick me. "On the bed, silly. You can't do it standing there."

Silence now as she moves to the doing of it. As she bends. I pull my knees back. How delicious it is. The pleasing. How delicious to be pleased. And they do like it. The girls are born to it. One must keep the order of things. I feel the heat of her mouth. I shall languish under the heat of a sucking mouth. Pity she isn't a man with bush whiskers to tickle me. She washes me now. Her tongue washing my garden. Her tongue fluttering in the groove. There is truth in the fluttering. Now she thinks of nothing but the pleasure of it. She will talk to the other girls about me. The girls will giggle as they talk of me. As they whisper how nice it is. This one with English blue eyes. Her girlish breasts. I wonder if Edward has had her yet. What an immense pleasure it must be to put the cock to such a girl, to hold her waist as she bends. Does she wail when he does it? How extravagant he is. The way he dotes upon his expensive collections. I would see him poke this girl. I would watch the mystery of it, the taking, the stretching of her pink flesh. How sweet she is. How silent she is in her devotions. Does she do the same to Claire? Yes, of course, the maids are Claire's possessions. I should like to see this girl licking my sister's jewel. I should like to see the familiarity of it. Perhaps the maid does it while Edward is watching. I ought to pay more attention to the sounds. I ought to catch them at it through the grate. If only Ellen Terry might warn me. But of course Miss Terry has been struck dumb by the sight of the heavens. One of our finest actresses, the clerk said. Her face and clothes. I would like to touch her. I would like to see her naked. And Edward. Where is Edward now? If he had any sense, he'd be here in this room to amuse me. Claire doesn't know how Edward amuses me. She doesn't know me. She doesn't know me at all. Her eyes see nothing. Sometimes she looks so foreign, so completely un-English. She ought to wear gold earrings. And this maid. She's clever, this one. A palpable difference exists between them. Dobbin is boring, Perkin is stupid, Selby is clever. Edward is clever also. I do hope they refuse that pompous party in Belgravia. I don't want to go. I don't want to go with Walter Bramsby to that pompous party. Does Edward understand that? He looks at me with such lust in his eyes. It's very bad for him. Sooner or later Claire will see it and we'll have a great row in the house. I don't want a row. Lord, what a tongue she has. Here we are. Well, darling, here it is. I can hear it now. The sounds of her lips. Barely preceptible. The licking. What a grand tragedy if Claire discovers me with Edward. Is this a pastoral grouping? Lady and her maid upon a bed of grass in Surrey. No, it's not Surrey, it's Kensington. In Claire's house in Kensington. How cozy it is. I don't think Claire cares for me. She says she does, but I don't think she does. Not as much as Selby does. The girl's tongue is truly marvelous. The zest. One feels on the verge of a new truth. She has me languishing. What can it mean? Perhaps it means I want Edward more than I think. He's not in a good temper these days. Lord, the girl is greedy. She wants me to die. She will take the life from me. All the servants want us to die. She feeds upon me. Now I'm nothing but a ripe fruit for a servant girl. One is as bad as the other. What does it matter when one is as bad as the other. Now, darling, now. The tongue at my bud. Her lips. Dear

God, the sweetness of a sucking kiss.

* * *

Edward has me in a corridor.

"You must come with me."

"Where?"

"To the library. Quickly, Julie."

He whispers at me. Once inside the library, he closes the door and whispers again. Claire is in the house. He's completely mad. He whispers about a place in Bloomsbury. A rendezvous. How silly he is. He insists. His eyes devour me. We shall be alone in Bloomsbury. He talks of love. It's madness to talk of love. I must make an effort to bring him to his senses. He pines at me.

"I slept very little last night."

"You have a wife."

"That's absurd and you know it."

"Well, what do you want?"

"I'll give you address. I'll be there at two in the afternoon tomorrow."

"It's impossible."

"Darling, it's the only way."

How ridiculous he is. Claire will discover us soon enough. Perhaps she knows it now. I think Edward has been drinking too much. Am I too cruel to him? Claire seems so high-spirited now.

"It's naughty of you."

He smiles. "I can't bear another day without you."

It's quite new to me. This eruption of fervor when the danger is so clear. I thought he'd be more discreet. I thought he was someone else. I tell him he's behaving like a silly schoolboy. "You know what I mean."

He looks pitiful. His eyes are so pitiful when they

look at me. I smile to make him happy again. Flirtation to make him happy again. A long glance at the front of his trousers that sets him muttering. The real point is the pleasure of it. I knew the danger in the very beginning. Shall I wear drawers to our rendezvous. One makes an attempt at sincere decorum. Nearby on the wall is a photograph of a man in uniform.

"Who's that?"

"My father," Edward says. 'My father in the Crimea."

* * *

He has something in Bedford Way, a bed-sitting room furnished in the dullest brown. How amusing to be at a trysting place. But of course it's more sensible than the house. He already has the fever in his eyes. He imagines me naked in his arms. Has he had other women here? "I've brought champagne," he says.

Poor Edward is so predictable. All these schoolboys who grow up to be predictable in their pleasures. The male heirs. He's a male heir.

"I don't know why."

"What?"

"I don't know why you've brought champagne."

"To celebrate, of course."

Am I menacing? I suppose not a soul knows about this place. Edward's room in Bloomsbury. Now he pours the wine and talks again. Some silly friend who wants to sit in Parliament. Edward is too young to have this room. He's too young at forty. A room like this belongs to a man of sixty, a man with full whiskers and a penchant for small girls in pink. Then Edward talks of going abroad again. To Italy. He talks of Florence with such distinction.

"Do stop."

"Stop?"

"Do stop talking."

I tell him I shall be busy all day tomorrow. And the day after that. Perhaps for another week. He holds his glass aloft. "Then we must have today."

"Are you an agnostic?"

"Julie, please . . ."

I'm sure it's more than I deserve. I don't deserve Claire's husband. "We're expected at home."

"You promised . . ."

I should adore it. I want to be civil to him. I suffer from total boredom, but I want to be civil. We sip our champagne. There will be so much to remember. A lifetime of remembrances.

He smiles again. "Darling, don't be so mysterious."

"Is she pretty?"

"Is who pretty?"

"The woman who was here last. I think that's a stocking half under the bed."

He curses the maid as he kicks at the stocking. Then he's upon me. He forces me upon the bed. I laugh as he pushes me down. His lips press against mine. My laughing as he kisses me. His tickling touches. His hand pushes beneath my dress. He touches my thighs. His fingers tickling along the insides of my thighs. Pulling at my garters. Then his lips are away and his head moves down. His head beneath my dress. The fortress besieged. Now the dress pushed up.His face between my thighs. I groan as I yield. Yes, that. I always want that. The hot kiss in my secret place. A sound of discovery now as he finds I have no drawers. How naughty I am. All the way in a cab from the house. Claire wanted me to have the carriage, but I insisted I wouldn't. How hungry he is. He delights in it. He's completely starved for it. I don't know why. She has him do it often enough. The tickling of his tongue. The way he forages in my nest. Oh yes, there. Sucking at my clitoris. I shall spend if he keeps on with that. He does know how. One must trust a lover to know how. He murmurs against my thighs. So much for the fidelity of marriage. He's had other women here. On this bed. His mouth feeding at others. Jealous, darling? Festivities in full swing now. Claire's Edward sucking at my copse with such devotion. I try to look. Nothing but a glimpse of his tongue. Pity I can't see all of it. Pity his face must be hidden. The hairs tickling his nose. Oh, get on with it. I feel I could swoon. Lying here under him, under his mouth, his lips. How charming he is when he twitches his mouth. One always thinks of the connection. His eagerness. He's better than a maid. His tongue flitting. He must find me copious. I can tell by the noise that I must be copious.

Then he wants me undressed. He pulls at my clothes.

"Don't be rude."

"Darling, please . . ."

"I'll do it myself. And you too."

We face each other across the bed as our clothes fall away. His fingers fumble. I ought to have a maid. Soon I stand in my chemise and Edward shows his appendages. His cock and balls. His penis rampant. He please with me to regain the bed. He wants me kneeling. He wants my rump in his hands. He fondles me. His mumbled admiration. I like the hot words. I like exposing things. How shocking it is to be exposed to his eyes. His penis is so stiff. He's a pompous man with a stiff pego. Generously endowed. Exquisite coloring. I want to see it, but he remains behind me with his hands on my bottom. These antics. I would like to be in a room full of gilt chairs. Bending to be examined by a collection of ambassadors. I hide nothing. Let them see the full measure of it.

Edward's fingers now. His knob pushing in. The stretching. He fills me. A slow thrusting. Thank God the bed doesn't creak. How appalling it would be if the bed creaked. I want to please him. I want to please that agitated limb he has. I find his balls. I hold his cods as I look at the room. At the dressing table. Perhaps there's another stocking beneath the dressing table. I will make him tell me. I shall make him tell everything.

Now his finger is at my rose-hole. He wants something more serious. I protest. "I won't allow it."

"Why not?"

"You're much too large."

"That's nonsense."

"Edward, I don't want it."

"I have some oil."

He insists. His root remains inside me as he reaches for the oil upon the night-table. My rose-hole fingered. Oiled. Then his root withdrawn. He's in a frenzy now and I must allow it. Then pushing again. This time at my bottom-hole. The entrance. Pushing, Stretching. His urgency. I'm like a maid before her master. Oh, the pleasure of it. His twitching root in my bottom. Always with John. The sliding. Edward is so firm. A slow stroking. He's quite perfect. One blesses perfection. My body sways. He mutters. He seems dazzled. One must have courage. I remain still. Bent like an animal. I pretend insouciance. Pretend, pretend. This is not Kensington, this is Bloomsbury, darling. In Edward's room. His belly slapping against the flesh of my bottom. His sharp cut nose. He's well-made. Considerable girth. One always feels it more in the back. His cods. My fingers at his cods. How perfect it is. Always moving. This extraordinary delight. And then his cry of pleasure. The final thrusting. The groaning. One takes them in the groaning.

* * *

"I had an awful time getting away."

He looks at me. The second time is more sedate. "But you did."

"Edward, we can't go on endlessly like this. Claire will see it."

I stand off from him. He wants me to undress. His passion is always at a boil. I demand some wine. I mount my courage. I rue the day I moved into that house in Kensington. Now I'm here again, once again in this room, once again in a dither of anticipation. He talks again. A rise in his voice. All our lives we shall remember this room. His bearing. I put him off.

"I wasn't fond of what you did last time."

He stands back. "I don't believe it."

"It's true."

"You did enjoy it."

"Oh Edward."

His illusions. His triumph. How do I manage his triumph. This false victory they have. He's English, after all. Not French. What an abomination it is to see him triumphant. I will keep my composure.

His vague stare. "You did like it."

"Is that what you want?"

"Yes, why not?"

I tease him. "It's not dignified."

"Good Lord."

I feel genuine affection for him. He's like a helpless boy. His temper on occasion. The memories of him with Claire. I kiss him again and he puts his hand on my bottom.

"You like my bottom too much."

"Let me see it."

I touch his mouth. "Will you kiss it?"

The fire in his eyes. He lies on his back on the rug. My dress lifted. Without drawers again. I show myself first. I feel his eyes burning. Then I descend. I descend upon his face.

One deals with a certain solicitude, traditions, mutterings on the Embankment. Nothing compares to certain supreme pleasures. His mouth wet. The feel of his mouth at the shrine. The feel of him breathing under me. How silent he is. No more silly talk of his collections. It's a well-ordered room. I move. I carry out my searching. His tongue. His doings in my bottom. How lively he is. Yes, I'm pleased. Rolling now. He does adore it. Luring him there. It's a wonder he can breathe. His nose in the quick as I settle down. He does like it. Oh yes, he does. I shall have more wine afterward. I shall have more wine.

Part Two: Claire

Chapter Eight

I DALLY IN MY ROOM with Dobbin the maid. I lie upon the chaise and Dobbin kneels beside me with her face at my belly. Her tongue flutters between my nether-lips. Her fingers tickle my thighs. The windows are open and I can hear the birds in the garden, the chirping of the birds, an occasional buzz of an insect, the soft slurping of Dobbin at my fountain. There is nothing in this room but tranquility.

And yet I'm restless. Despite the languid mood, I feel agitated. It's always like this, always the agitation. Is it the maid? Dobbin's face is flushed. Her attention is fixed upon my exposed belly, my open thighs, my sex. Would she rather I be on the bed? When I called her to my room, she arrived with a shy smile. She's accustomed to me now. After three years in the house, she knows my ways. A maid ought to know the ways of her mistress. She knows I don't like her to be gloomy. She knows I like her to be playful. She giggles as I close my thighs about her head. She pretends to be smothered. I open my thighs. She breathes again. She kisses my sex again. How eager she is. She nuzzles between my nether-lips. Her tongue continually flutters.

I must make a supreme effort to be at ease. What a pity not to enjoy the work of a girl like this. Such delights. She has an appetite for it. Certain maids come into service and one quickly sees they have no yearning for it. And then at the first bidding they hold back. They weep. Nothing is more disgusting than a weeping maid. One wants only silence from a servant. I don't like it when they weep. Dobbin never weeps. Dobbin is never unpleasant. She has full lips. She pulls at my clitoris with her full lips. I'm so tired. I feel malicious. I want to push her away and at the same time I want the sucking to be more firm. I don't like her maid's cap. I don't like her eyes when she looks at me. I don't like to be looked at when they do it. I wonder what they think. I wonder what they tell each other in their murky little rooms. Of course they talk about us. Myself and Edward and my sister. Whispering in the kitchen ever since the arrival of my sister. The pretty one. I suppose they call her the pretty one. Julie has such lovely hair. Is she comfortable in her room? Oh yes, she is. My sister is most certainly comfortable in her room. She has that photograph of Ellen Terry and behind the photograph is the grate and through the grate she spies upon me. She watches me. She watches everything that happens in this room. She's not watching now because now she's not in the house. But if she were in the house she would watch me again. How amusing it is. Ellen Terry. What a perfect little goose of an actress she is. The grate ought to be covered by someone more substantial. If she doesn't like those roses, she ought to have found something more suitable than Ellen Terry. It's completely ridiculous to have Ellen Terry on that wall. I suppose she thinks it's a humorous touch. I suppose she thinks it's an adventure to spy on me through the grate. Does she smile? I hate it when she smiles. I think her face looks so common when she smiles. One doesn't want a smiling sister. That evening at the Cosmo when she laughed at Walter. Poor Walter is so much alone. Of course Julie wouldn't understand that. She might confess to other things, but not to that. So dense behind that pretty face. Entangled in her secrets. She was never happy as a married woman. She thought I didn't know, but I knew perfectly well she wasn't happy. She can't hide something like that from her own sister. It's not possible. And now what sort of future will she have? John not here. Drowned in the gondola of that lovely balloon. How awful it was when the news came. One never thinks of it. The question never appeared. And then one discovers there's more to life than a jolly good time. What a formidable man he was. Oh dear yes. I do remember him. There are men one doesn't forget. John will not be forgotten. Except perhaps by Julie. I don't think she ever had much affection for him. My sister is the happiest widow I've ever known. She doesn't hide the truth of it. Husband dead in watery grave and her with not much to show for it except a few newspaper clippings. If she has the clippings. Which I doubt. I do know my own sister. One always knows certain things. Pity she isn't watching me now. I might look at the grate and make a face. Shock her into a state of grace as she understands I know about the grate. Of course I know about it. I do live in this house. I live in this house and that's the mouth of one of my maids down there. Dobbin's pretty little full-lipped mouth. Dobbin's lovely kisses. The room is so pleasant when the windows are thrown open. I feel her breath. She knows I don't like to have it rushed. It's hateful when it's rushed. One doesn't want to rush it. One wants a deliberate dalliance. Last Sunday I had her kiss my evening shoes a full five minutes before she ever touched my legs. One wants discretion in a maid.

Edward, of course, says that Dobbin is too dull. He likes them a bit more plump. More flesh in the breast and buttock. Like Julie, I suppose. The two of them. The double perfidy. She imagines my ignorance. She imagines I know nothing of it. How silly she is. I know everything. That flat he has in Bedford Way. They take pleasure in their deception. My sister and my husband. She's always lived without guilt. She has no thought of any loyalty to anyone but herself. She's a scheming wretch. One sees girls like her in the music halls. Commonplace tarts with jiggling bosoms. I shudder when I think of my past life. Julie always in the shadows. Father's imbecility. The way he doted on her. Their secret doings. I have a thousand memories of his hand fondling her bottom. She does have lovely breasts. Like those tropical melons we had in Naples. Nipples jutting so obscenely. I'm sure Edward adores them. I'm sure he's dreamt about breasts like that during all the years of our marriage. His fantasies of harem women. What a marvelous thing it would be to see them together. His mouth sucking at her bovine teats. Does she ever think of me when he does it? Or John? Or is everything forgotten. All the forgetting one does in the heat of it. Edward is so insistent with his women. I should like to see her brought to tears, but of course it won't happen. One must accept the realities of one's life. I shall be amused by my knowledge of it. They way they danced at the Cosmo. It doesn't matter. I won't have her thinking me unhappy. She must understand perfectly the way things are. I shall avoid any embarrassing situations. I detest embarrassing situations. Edward can be so boastful at times. My life seems to consist of maneuvering between one sticky moment and another. All the secrets. What a misfortune it is to know all the secrets.

Now I push at Dobbin's head. She looks up at me, her face flushed, her mouth wet. "Madam?"

"Tell me about her. Tell me about my sister."

"Your sister, Madam?"

"Yes, my sister, you ninny. What do you do with her?"

The girl's eyes are worried. She makes a sound in her throat. "Please, madam . . ."

I insist. I insist she tell me everything. "Do you suck her breasts?"

The maid wipes her mouth with her skirt. Her eyes are glazed. She nods. "Sometimes she wants that."

"And what else?"

"Mostly it's down there." Her eyes upon my sex. My belly is still uncovered, my nether-lips unfurled.

"Does she like it? Do you make her spend?"

The girl blushes. Her full lips show the merest beginning of a smile. "She always does."

* * *

Edward favors Perkin. We sit in the drawing room, Edward and I, and when the maid is called she seems uneasy.

"Edward, have you been unkind to her?"

"Certainly not."

"I won't have you unkind to them. We can't keep them if you don't use some common sense."

"Claire, darling, it's a maid."

"Yes, I know it's a maid. I can see she's a maid. Anyone can see that, for heaven's sake."

"I mean it's only maid."

"I don't want the bother of replacing them each year."

"Quite so."

He folds his hands upon his knee. Julie is out. The maid's eyes are uncertain. She thinks: What this time? Oh, I do understand them. Their girlish brains filled with nothing but silly fancies.

Edward beckons to the girl with his hands. His hands waving at her to come forward. She moves with hesitation. A glance at my chair. Yes, I shall remain in audience.

"Perkin?"

"Yes, madam?"

"I don't want you to look at me."

"Yes, madam."

She has a generous bottom, this one. I suppose that's why he finds her appealing. She stands before him. He says nothing. He motions with his fingers and she begins lifting her skirt. Her legs appear, her black cotton stockings, the white skin of her thighs. She has pretty legs. She blushes as she reveals her cotton drawers. Her eyes are lowered. Are there tears in her eyes? Edward fumbles with her drawers, his hand in the folds, his cheeks pink. The drawers come down, sliding down to the girl's ankles. She shows a full nest, dark, a thick bush at the joining of her thighs. Holding her skirt at her waist, she steps out of her drawers and remains still again. I see her in profile. Her full bottom thrusting out in its roundness. Edward makes her turn. Now she has her back to him. He touches her bottom. Just his fingertips. He uses both hands to feather the undersides of the two globes. Her rounds. His fingers move away to stroke her hips, then return again to the creasing between her globes and thighs. Now he pulls. He parts the two hemispheres. His eyes hot. I do know the look. His eyes hot as he examines her rear portal. His focus. He always takes them there. The maids are worth nothing to him but for that. And of course by now the girls know it. There is never any doubt that when Edward call it means a rose-hole corked. Do they giggle when they talk of it? He drops his hands now. He murmurs. He tells her to strip. Her fingers fumble with the strings. In a few moments she stands before him wearing nothing but her stockings and a white maid's cap that barely covers her chignon. Her charms revealed. She's a mere servant, after all. One sees it in the strong legs, the broad hips, the nipples like thick udders waiting for the infant. A country girl. What a stupid thing she is. She ought to have stayed in the north country. What a stupid girl to come to the city for this.

Edward unbuttons his trousers. He brings his tool out. His pink cock. The head blushing. The girl drops to her knees and takes his root in her hand. I've seen it all before. Every detail, all he gestures. The movements following one another in a slow procession. First her fingers, her fingertips dancing along his length. Then her lips at the tip. Her mouth opens. She engulfs his knob. His eyes upon her face. His face flushed as he watches her. She sucks with abandon. She makes no attempt to hide her gluttony. Her broad rump sways as she sucks him. When I was young I thought the maids were beaten into submission. They are not beaten. They are cajoled. Then after they are cajoled, they are willing. One can see the willingness in the way she fills her mouth with his flesh. How fascinating it is. The girl's mouth stretched by my husband's tool. I've had it in my body. I've had it probing in all the expected places. Now he fills the girl's mouth, stretches her lips, her mouth moving as she stuffs herself. She sucks and licks. Her tongue works. How practical the tongue is. Her young mouth. I do like to watch it. I like the simplicity of it. The swollen flesh stretching her lips. Of course Julie takes him this way. She has such a rapacious mouth. My sister. She bites him with her teeth. I suppose Edward adores Julie's mouth. She has a pretty mouth. Curling lips. A mouth to promote expectations of pleasure. Look how Edward perspires now. His forehead gleaming. Is it that warm in the room? Or has he lost his equanimity to a servant girl? What an annoyance. In the girl's mouth. Her eyes are closed. Sometimes one sees hatred in the eyes. A glint. Emphemeral. It quickly passes to be replaced by a placid look. I don't like to abuse the servants. We haven't come to that. It's not at all necessary, is it? What does it matter if there's an occasional rebellion in the kitchen? What a marvelous rump she has. Big in the bottom. She's anxious for it now. She hopes it's not too late. I shall sip my tea and watch it. I shall drink my tea and watch my husband and a servant girl.

Now Edward pushes her away. The girl's mouth is wet. Her face is flushed. He tells her to stand at the armchair and show her bottom. Her plump flesh jiggling as she moves. The clock chimes the hour. Tranquility in the drawing room. Edward and I in our drawing room. Perkin is the center of attention. The maid wearing only her black cotton stockings. Edward tells her to bend. She bends. Her arms forward to hold the armchair. She moves her legs apart as she bends further. Her pouch is visible, the hairy nest, the fat lips of her young sex.

Edward rises and goes to her. His root protrudes out of his trousers. He puts his hands on her bottom. He fondles her. He glances at me and smiles. His contented smile. Then he looks at the girl's rump again. He looks at her rose-hole. He has such a passion for it. He strokes it with a finger. He pushes his finger inside and the girl moans as he pulls the finger out again. A moan of expectation, isn't it? A tube of ointment appears from one of Edward's pockets. There is no sound except the ticking of the clock as he anoints the girl's aperture. When the task is finished, Edward replaces the tube in his pocket and removes his coat. He stands in his waistcoat and shirtsleeves. He unbuttons the lower buttons of his waistcoat and unhooks his braces. His trousers fall, then his drawers. His apparatus dangles. Cock and balls in a thicket of hair. He handles his balls as if to test their fullness. Then his hand returns to the girl's bottom. His finger pushes in again. He stretches the ring. Perkin groans as he works the finger inside. The girl shudders.

"Edward, don't hurt her."

He turns his eyes to me. I hear the ticking of the clock on the mantelpiece. The curtains move. A smell of spring coming in through the open window. Edward smiles at me. "She's perfect. Not small. I don't like it when they're too small."

His finger is withdrawn. He turns his hand to use his thumb. First the ball of his thumb on the girl's rose-hole. Then his thumb pushing inside. Perkin moans again. Now Edward's other fingers are free to touch her sex. To push inside. He fills her two apertures with his fingers. A wailing sound comes out of the girl's throat. He likes them spending. She sways her hips, her white globes moving from side to side. Her thighs are plump above the tops of her stockings. Edward's fingers continue moving. He lingers. How he lingers.

At last his fingers come out and he points his tool at the ring. He pushes in. Perkin moans. He pushes further. Steady in the pushing. His eyes upon it. His root sliding inside her fundament. The girl groans continually. Her legs tremble. Edward lifts his eyes. He waits. Except for the movement of his hands on her rump, one would say he had an air of detachment. His brow is wrinkled. I wonder about his thoughts. How futile it is to wonder about his thoughts. It's quite another thing to have them told at dinner. He has such a clever ability to evade inconvenient questions. His face will assume a look of complete gravity. Then a moment later his features will change and his look will be boisterous. During our honeymoon, his transformations were unpredictable. My mother promised me I would be happy. She said Edward would make a fine husband.

Now he grips the maid's bottom as he starts to

move. He pumps at her bottom, a slow and even pumping. Unhurried. The girl wriggles. I can see the joining. Edward's tool is quite big. The girl has a splendid bottom. Her rose-hole is enormously stretched. He moves easily. There is no forcing. She warbles. Her legs are shaking. I raise my gown to my thighs. I find my sex with my hand. My fur. My fingers in my furry place. I stroke myself. I stroke my clitoris as I watch them. I like the watching of it. The sliding tool. The grasping ring. How perfect it is. The girl's bottom is marvelous. Edward now shows the pleasure in his face. His eyes are bright. He watches the sliding. My sex is weeping. My fingers work in the wet. Perkin's face is hidden, but I suppose she wears a sweet smile.

Are we in a state of decay? When I was a girl I wanted my life confined to a garden of white roses. I had no thoughts of ambitious undertakings. I did not like the crowds in the exhibition halls in Paris. The only men I knew were old. All the others were unknown. I had all the comforts and I wanted them to endure. One always wants the comforts.

Does Edward have his comforts? His hands move over the girl's rump as he continues pumping in her bottom. I can see the swing of his balls. My fingers are in a fury as I watch them. My husband and this girl. My marriage. He makes a sound. He presses against her as he spends. I watch the shuddering. The cleaving. Edward and the maid.

* * *

In the evening I am alone with Edward in my bedroom. No, not alone. The eyes are there. Julie's eyes at the grate. Does Edward know? His face is so placid. He does not know about the grate. And Julie is not aware that I know she watches us. An entanglement of deceptions.

"Edward, what do you think of her?"

He looks at me. "Think of whom?"

"My sister, darling. What do you think of my sister?"

"I don't know what you mean."

"You haven't really known her before. Now that she lives with us, what do you think of her?"

"She's pleasant enough."

"Do you find her beautiful? I've always thought Julie was extremely pretty."

"She's quite good-looking."

"Yes, of course."

"It's in the family."

"You don't mean that."

"Yes I do."

"Do you think she ought to marry Walter Bramsby?"

"I don't know. If she wants to, I suppose she ought to."

"Edward, you're always so vague. Do you want to undress me? You may as well do it now."

I stand before the mirror as Edward undresses me. His fingers are nimble. His hands work at my clothes. My gown falls, then my chemise and drawers. Edward smiles as he looks at my breasts and belly. He bends to retrieve my clothes, to help me step out of them. His fingers trail over my legs, along my stockings. He fondles my calves and then my thighs. I am sure Julie is watching us. I shall not look at the grate. I shall not allow her to have any suspicion of my knowing.

Edward remains upon his knees. He presses his face against my legs. He mumbles. I suppose I ought to be angry about the grate. Her watching. I think of the past. One hates to shed tears about the past. It seems so useless. I think of those last days in

Paris before I left for England. The last day. The last one. Julie tearful in my arms. What does she think about when she holds Edward in her arms? Is she jealous of the servants? One never knows the truth of things. Edward has such a saintly look when he kneels at my feet. My husband is an image of devotion. I can see desire in his face, in his eyes. I suppose some might say it is Satan in his eyes. My mother. Mother never understood the essence of things. How shameless Edward was in the very beginning.

I cover my breasts. My two small birds. I wonder what he thinks of me when he's with her. One always wonders. Now he fondles my legs. He looks at my belly, my sex. He likes me naked. I see the liking in his eyes. What a pity that Julie's eyes are hidden. I should like to see her eyes. I turn. I present my bottom to Edward. We drank champagne this evening and I suppose he's a bit drunk. He always kneels when he's had too much to drink. I don't mind it. I like the kneeling. His face now. He kisses my bottom. He kisses in the crevice while my sister watches. He kisses me under the nasty eyes of my sister.

Then his kissing stops. I turn. Edward rises and removes his dressing gown. He stands naked before me. His cheeks are pink. His eyes are shining. He murmurs as I fondle him. I hold the weight of his balls in my hand. I squeeze his tool. He likes the fondling. I can see in his face that he likes the fondling. We stand in profile to the grate. Let Julie see. Does she fondle him like this? Does she pull at his tool with her fingers? I must not show any anger. I must not deny their silly aspirations. They amuse themselves with deception. Julie has her triumph. Edward has his lust. I have only my apathy. His cock in my hand is so thick and hot. How he burns in his lust. I hold his throbbing tool. My finger stroking him. I am his wife. I have the torment. Is Julie the virtuous one? Oh, please spare me the madness of it. She ought to marry Walter Bramsby. She ought to regain her place in society. Edward trembles now. I'm fond of teasing him. One must never misjudge one's husband. His knob is so impatient. His balls seem to grow in my hand. Can Julie see him growing? Can she see all of the room? Edward looks pale in the yellow light. Can she see everything?

On the bed now. My thighs are open. Edward's eyes are upon my belly. I raise my knees and he comes to me. His face slides to my source. His mouth covers my sex. I wriggle beneath his tongue. I want her to watch it. I want her to see his tongue. I open my nether-lips with my fingers. How ridiculous he is with his tongue wagging at me. He mumbles. Then silence as he sucks. His lips pull at my flesh. This is the only thing of importance. His mouth upon me beneath the lamp. To have my sister watch it. His nose pushing at me. He talks of his friends at his club and I always wonder what they do with their women. Mrs. Grantham and Mrs. Dovedale. Mrs. Pallant and Mrs. Ashbury. Their clothes are always in fashion. The way they boast of the accomplishments of their husbands. All the boasting that's been done in this house. All the stupid dinner parties. I'm so innocent. In the midst of vulgar people I have no defense. I want to see her face. I want to see my sister's face as she watches us. What a joke it is. What a bitter tawdry joke it is. My knowledge of it. My knowledge of her watching.

I push Edward away. He roles onto his back like a wax mummy. I mount him. I take his tool inside my sex. I ride him. Riding a St. George. His eyes are glazed. I pray she can see it. I want her to see the joining. I want her to watch my riding. He holds my haunches with his hands. Is she surprised at my vigor? What a delight it is to ride like this. I see the happiness in Edward's eyes. Does he adore me? We have unpleasant moments. We have our good times and bad times. We have our evasions. We have our convictions. We have a refuge in each other. After all the tedium, one at least has a refuge.

Now I pull away, drop his tool out of my sex and turn to have his face. I settle down. Wriggling as I find his nose in the crevice. Wriggling again to get his mouth at my fountain. Pushing down. His tongue inside. The shifting a bit to get his tongue in the other place. The pleasure of it. He does adore it. I suppose he does it with her. I suppose she knows the madness of his tongue in her rose. Yes, he does the same. He groans now in the pleasure. I squirm upon his face. I hold his tool as he spends. His effusion bursting. The way he spurts. I quiver as I touch the scattered pearls. This one is for Julie. I touch it with my forefinger. This one belongs to my darling sister.

Chapter Nine

WALTER BRAMSBY FINDS ME in a confection shop in Oxford Street. He insists we go somewhere for tea. He has a plate of Italian cakes brought to the table for me. He proclaims me to be the loveliest woman in the room. "And Julie's sister. How wonderful to know you both."

"She's the lovely one."

"I find you both enchanting."

"Dear Walter."

He looks pensive. "I do love her, you know. She's a marvelous thing, isn't she? An extraordinary woman."

"You've told her, of course."

"Oh yes. I'm filled with hope. I can't think of anything else these days. I want so much to be her husband."

"I'll be pleased to have you as a brother-in-law, provided you continue offering these delicious Italian cakes."

"I think she'd be the most loyal wife. That's quite important these days, isn't it?"

"Yes, I suppose it is."

"I want . . . love from a woman. Surprised, aren't you? You didn't expect that from me."

"Not really."

"But it's what I want. That's really what I want. Something that lasts. A great passion. And I think Julie is capable of it. Most women aren't, you know. She's the first woman I've known who I think could rise to it. A great passion."

"How lovely."

"I have the feeling I know her so well. Sometimes I think we've met before . . . in our dreams."

"Walter, darling . . ."

"No, don't make fun."

"I'm not making fun. I hadn't realized how romantic you are."

"I'm in love with your sister and I intend to marry her."

"Well, then I suppose you shall."

"If she'll have me. I do think she'll have me."

"I think she's quite fond of you."

"It's as if I've been keeping myself for her. My wife. Oh yes. It's fate, isn't it? She told me that at one point after John was lost she thought of returning to France forever. We'd never have met. I don't like travelling. I'm never comfortable out of England. Too much the Englishman and all that. And how would I find her? So you see, it must something ordered by the stars."

"How poetic you are."

"She smiles when I say it. But I can always see in her eyes that she thinks as I do. I can always see it." He touched his lips. "You must think I'm silly."

"I certainly don't think that."

"There are practicalities, aren't there? She needs looking after and I've the means. Quite enough, I suppose. Although of course one never has enough, does one?"

"Perhaps not."

He laughed softly. "Money is quite important, isn't it?"

"Yes, I should think so."

"I don't like all this talk against money. All this nonsense about the rich. The rich put order in the world and then nasty names are thrown at them. Well, what can one expect from the rabble? Now they want porters and lift-boys to have weekends. You don't dislike money, do you? It's not French, is it?"

Now it was I who laughed. "I don't think so."

"Do you mind? Do forgive me. I shouldn't go on like that. Please say you forgive me."

"I forgive you."

"You're quite beautiful. If I weren't so madly in love with Julie, I think I should make a fool of myself in pursuit of you."

* * *

We meet again nearly a week later. This time Walter calls at the house for me and we drive in the park in a closed carriage. As before, he talks about Julie. Now he seems convinced she intends to reject him. "I think I see the signs of it. She's always affectionate, but I think I see the signs of it."

I soothe him. "I know she's fond of you."

"I don't think she wants me."

"Perhaps it's too soon after the loss of John."

"I'm terribly unhappy."

"My sister is so uncertain about things."

"Can you help me, Claire?"

"Walter, you must have patience."

"Please . . . .I beg you."

"I don't know what I can do."

"I'm sure you'll think of something."

How helpless he is. "I'll try, darling."

He begins to babble about his life. He talks about his loneliness. He talks about how much he needs her. "I think of her constantly. It's rather like a fever. I've never felt like this about a woman before. It's extraordinary. I hadn't thought it was possible. She's become the great passion of my life. I can't bear the thought of not having her as a wife. You will support me, won't you, Claire? She thinks highly of you. She always talks of how much she admires you."

"You must keep on with it. You must keep after

her, Walter. I'm certain you'll have what you want."

"Do you really think so?"

"Perseverence, darling."

"Yes, I think you're right."

"It might be useful to remind her of things."

"What things?"

"How much she needs you. How much she needs the comforts you can give her. I daresay a gift of some sort would be suitable."

"A necklace?"

"That's a marvelous idea. Quite perfect. Something elegant and at the same time romantic."

He beams. "I'll find something."

"Yes, you must. And I promise I'll talk to her. I'll press your case whenever I see the chance for it."

He bubbles with gratitude. "Claire, darling . . . I'll be in your debt forever. How marvelous it is to have your help. I must be the most fortunate man on earth. My life has been blessed by two extraordinary women. Parisian women. I think I'll now consider myself an eternal friend of France."

"But you must promise to keep trying."

"Yes of course."

I tell him he has excellent prospects. Julie needs a husband and he has all the qualities a woman might want in a man. How pleased he is. His eyes shine as he considers his future with Julie. And why not? If she has to marry someone, why not Walter Bramsby? His cheeks are flushed. He holds my hand and proclaims his indebtedness to me. As the carriage rolls on, he inundates me with gratitude. Once again he tells me he would pursue me were it not for his love for Julie. "How lovely you are."

I smile. "You'll make me blush."

"Do you really believe Julie will accept me?"

"You're a charming man and she'd be a fool not to."

"Do you really think so?"

"I suspect you're quite capable with women. You are, aren't you, Walter? Oh yes, I can tell."

He still holds my hand. He flatters me. He says I have the most beautiful eyes. He says I'm one of the few women who have ever understood him. How amusing he is. The way he babbles. I glance at the front of his trousers and find his arousal is evident. Is it Julie or myself? I believe it's me. I want it to be me. How lovely to have it me and not Julie. I glance at it boldly. I imagine I can see the throbbing. He pets my hand. I want to touch him but I refrain. No, not yet. Walter is such a child. One mustn't rush things. His breathing is heavy. His eyes dance as he chatters about some silly painting he's bought. I want to see his tool. I want him quivering as I stroke him, as I hold him in my hand. One wonders about dimensions. I think a man ought to be impressive. The vital part, of course. That's not silly, is it? I don't like disappointments. I like to have them extraordinary. Yes, extraordinary. Something to admire. Something sturdy. Definitely not puny. One doesn't want them puny. Thick around as my wrist and as long as can be. Claire, darling, you're losing your senses. How long? Oh dear, I couldn't say. Something substantial. One always wants something substantial.

"Do you kiss her?"

"Kiss her?"

I laugh. "Walter, darling, do you kiss Julie? You don't mind if I ask, do you?"

"No, not at all."

"Then you must tell me."

"The answer is yes."

"And what else? If I'm to be your confidante, you must tell me everything."

He groans. "Everything?"

"Yes, darling, everything. You must tell me everything."

He finally admits to it. The intimacy that exists between himself and my sister. The kissing. The touching. He blushes as he talks. He stammers. I laugh. "I was right about you. You're a man who mesmerizes women."

"It's not true."

"You've mesmerized my sister."

"Claire, I haven't. It's not like that at all."

"Do you make her swoon?"

"It's not like that."

"Then like what? What is it like? Tell me, Walter. Tell me everything. I won't let you refuse. I demand to know everything."

The truth slowly emerges. The kisses. The fondling of my sister's breasts. She allows him that. Walter stutters. I begin to understand it. She always has him lick her. He licks her until she spends. Then she milks him. She tells him she likes to watch the spurting. She always milks him with her hand.

"Is that enough? Don't you want more than that?"

He groans. How helpless he is. "I . . . really, Claire, it's not possible to discuss it."

"Kiss me."

"What?"

"I said kiss me."

His eyes are empty. His face moves towards mine. He kisses my lips. The kiss becomes warm. He feels my tongue. I press against him, intrude my tongue between his lips. He murmurs something. His arms enfold me. "Claire, darling . . ."

"Kiss me again."

Now the kiss is wet and deep. He groans against my lips. "Good Lord . . ."

"Don't you like it?"

"I adore it."

"Poor Walter. You do love Julie, don't you?"

"Yes."

"Then we should stop this."

"Claire, please . . ."

I touch his cheek. I glance down at the front of his trousers and he blushes as I smile. His arousal is evident. He babbles as I gaze at the evidence. How amusing he is. At full stand in his trousers. I tease him. I touch his coat, his waistcoat, the gold chain of his watch.

"Do you like it when Julie touches you?"

He makes a sound of assent.

"Then I shall do it also. You want me to, don't you? You must tell me you want it."

"Darling . . ."

I touch him. Tickling touches. My fingers tickling along the length of it through his trousers. He's quite substantial. Substantial enough. Well-proportioned. "Walter, I'm flattered."

His excitement is intense. "What an amazing woman you are."

"I think I've astonished you. Have I astonished you, Walter? Yes, I think I have."

His astonishment is complete in my hand. I feel the heat of it, the throbbing of his tool beneath my fingers. He shudders as I undo the buttons.

"Claire, I . . ."

"I want to see it."

"I feel as though I'm betraying Edward."

"Don't be silly."

And then I have it. His tool exposed. Pink. Firm. Quivering beneath my fingertips. Walter shudders. I kiss his lips again. I tease him. My fingers tickling. How childish he is. Like a large boy. He takes my free hand and kisses it. His lips upon my fingers.

One hand at his lips. The other hand clasping his urgency.

"Tell me about Julie."

"Julie?"

"What does she do? Does she stroke you like this? Up and down like this?"

I insist that he tell me. I want to know how she fondles him. He mumbles as he tells me. I have him tell me again. He says Julie's caresses drive him mad. He says she teases him until he feels at the brink of madness. When he's with her, it's almost as if she's cast a spell over him. He finds himself completely helpless. I imagine it. I have a complete image of it as I fondle his tool. She strokes him, milks him, toys with him. Then she has him kneeling at her feet. She has him nuzzling, sniffing at her drawers. She has him struggling to get at her. His hands at her drawers. Her sex finally revealed. He cries out as his mouth covers her. He groans as he feeds between her thighs.

"But you like it."

"I can't help it."

"Poor darling. My sister is so demanding, isn't she? She ought to be more gentle with you. My poor little darling."

How sturdy he is. The carriage rolls on. Walter gazes down at my stroking hand.

"It's frightening."

"Frightening, darling?"

"I keep thinking it's her. But it's not her. It's not Julie."

Most definitely not. I shall be annoyed at you if you confuse us."

"Claire, darling . . ."

"You mustn't think of her. Not now. Oh my, you're almost there, aren't you? Your handkerchief, darling. We don't want to soil your trousers, do we?"

His handkerchief appears. I cover his tool. A moment later he gasps as he spends. A deep groan. My hand continues moving. My fingers gripping him. He calls out as he spurts again. The words are too garbled to make them out.

* * *

Julie is uncertain. She sips her tea with a vagueness in her eyes. "I don't know if I want to again. I mean it's not necessary, is it?"

"Not necessary?"

"Well, yes, I suppose it is. I suppose I ought to do what people expect of me."

"Darling, you must do what makes you happy."

"I don't have anything. If I had something, I wouldn't. I don't really like it, you know. I don't like being a wife. Not when it's just ordinary. An ordinary marriage. The stupid hours. The dinner parties. I hate dinner parties. John always liked a full calendar of dinner parties."

"Oh dear."

"I think you ought to be thankful Edward isn't like that."

"Yes, I am."

"I don't know about Walter. Oh yes, I suppose he'd make a decent husband. I suppose I ought to. If he wants me. I suppose I ought to."

"Julie, he does want you."

"One wants to be settled."

"Yes, darling."

"I should like my own house, my own comforts."

"Don't you think it would best?"

"I don't know."

"Darling Julie."

"You see, I'm not certain of anything. It's awful,

isn't it?"

"I do think you ought to marry him."

"Will I be . . . happy? There were times when I wasn't quite happy with John. I never told you, did I? Well, one never tells everything. I'm not sure I even knew it. And if I didn't know it, I couldn't tell you, could I?"

"I suppose not."

"John could be so dull. Men do have the capacity for a monstrous dullness. So completely dull."

"On occasion."

"He was so fascinated with the ground as seen from his balloon. But down on the ground, he wasn't much of anything, was he? Is it horrible of me to say that? Down on the ground he wasn't much of anything at all."

Chapter Ten

PARIS IN MARCH WAS ALWAYS DREARY. I remember the grey afternoons in the drawing room, the clicking of Mother's knitting needles, the rattling of the window panes each time the wind beat against the house. Julie and I liked to sit near the fire and read. One carries the years of habit. Father often had an ill-temper. Mother was snobbish. We relished our silences. Might things have been different under a different spell? One never knows about different spells.

Julie and I often whispered together. We had our confidences. On occasion Mother showed her annoyance with our whispering. Mother refused exclusion from any aspect of life in the house.

Father liked to boast of the important people he knew. Figures in the Assembly. An occasional marquis. He never talked of their indiscretions. Only strangers were guilty of indiscretions. Father did not like to gossip. Mother would press him, but he would maintain his silence. He was a man who kept to his satisfactions. He was a man of long silences.

I had my moments of distress as a girl. I hated my life in that old house in Paris. I thought Julie's hands were prettier than mine. I hoped for a husband with plenty of money. I hoped I would not suffer disappointments. I wanted a life of refinement. I wanted the eyes of admiration when I attended church on the arm of my husband. I enjoyed a tight bodice. I conjured up a dashing past as the daughter of the Ambassador of Portugal. I conjured recollections. I conjured triumphs at elegant balls.

One day Edward appeared as a distinguished suitor. Father was uninterested: he yawned. But Mother whispered to me. She said the Englishman had a substantial income. She said he cut a handsome figure. She said I would know the love of a man of substance. She talked of the sentimentality of long engagements. None of it mattered to me except the promise of escape to an interesting life. A life of comfort and a plentitude of servants. I wanted a luxurious garden. I wanted a large house. I was impatient to have command of things. Edward and I went for long walks in the Tuileries. He talked of the London season. He talked of the furniture we would buy. He talked of the pleasures we would share. I tasted a life of satisfactions. How joyful it would be to be free of Paris. Sometimes Edward stroked my arm. We smiled at each other through afternoons of quiet intimacy. He promised my life would be an unending series of elegant amusements. He was so distinguished. A man of worldly experience, my mother said. She was in high spirits. She planned the announcement of the engagement. Julie pouted in a fit of envy. She pretended a crisis of melancholy. I withdrew from it all into a perfect propriety. Now I had to be a deliberate woman. What a splendid life I would have. Edward was an only son and all his family's estates had passed down to him. Mother made a play at sadness at the prospect of my leaving her. Father said nothing. I think he disliked Edward. I think he was annoyed that Edward seemed so completely at ease. Father withdrew. He made no attempt to interfere with Mother's management of things. Mother bustled in her management. She complained of an arthritic hand as she made her lists. Her nose pushed and pointed and insisted. She took great delight in snubbing certain acquaintances. She said I should have a glorious wedding. Truly glorious, she said. Edward's family will be impressed. We must make a very good impression. She said I must understand the realities. She said it was futile to convince people of anything, but impressions always mattered. I had moments of burning doubt. Then the doubt would vanish as I fussed with my trousseau. I ignored Mother's pretentions. She had the ability to provoke a swooning despair, an agony of despair. I felt a great hatred for her. I wanted control of my life. As Edward's wife I should have a new power. I should escape those stupid evenings staring at the Seine. Was I too thin? I would not listen to any coaxing. My father's eyes seemed glazed with his tedium. And I had my own tedium. The engagement seemed interminable. Edward was such a lazy suitor. Restrained. No more than idle touchings in the park. Flowers and sweets. He presented me with what he said was the purest diamond in Paris. Mother showed such eagerness as she examined it. She wagged her head at my father, chiding him for his indifference. I remembered the time Julie and I had watched them at the farm. Mother bending. Mother upon her knees and Father behind her. Her broad white bottom in Father's hands. Now she sat sniffing in her pretended primness, her knitting needles clicking as she spoke with sarcasm of my father's family.

Julie was not happy at my betrothal. She was envious. I delighted in her envy. She accused me of whispering to my friends about her. She said we were sisters and I ought not to whisper about her. She hated the attention I received. Mother chuckled in her amusement. She said I was too undisciplined. She said my future husband would teach me the English ways. She said I ought to have the right frame of mind when I went to England. What a lovely chance I had! She talked of all her years in the bosom of Paris.

Julie and I had our secrets. I was envious of Julie's hair. Now my sister is in my life again. She sleeps in a room next to mine. In my husband's house. Edward talks in the drawing room. We all talk. I must listen beyond the babble of the talking. I must learn the intentions. It's much too dangerous to be oblivious to things. There are two of them in the house now. How does he do it to her? How does he take her? I want to see it. I want to see her bent like a maid. I want to see Edward's cock in my sister's quim. I want to see the doing of it. Does she suck him? I want to see his knob in her mouth. Her stretched lips. His thrusting tool. I think of them. I imagine them. I suppose he buys her presents. Edward is a man who likes to buy his women presents.

I ought to be furious at them. Must I be angry? One ought not to tolerate deception. How deceiving she is. She parades with an air of simply gaiety, but how deceiving she is. And Edward is so dull. A woman always understands her husband better than she understands any other man. Edward pleasures himself with my sister. In his dullness. One imagines his dull eyes as he does it. I am his wife. Am I his wife? In truth, I have no connection to him beyond the vows. My husband. Without his money, what would he be? What would he be to me? They sit at the dinner table each evening with duplicity in their eyes. Edward's lying eyes. How stupid of them to believe I do not know. How surprising that Julie hasn't guessed. Is she bemused by him? He's not that clever. I know Edward well enough to know how clever he is. Julie is the clever one. A woman must be clever to bring off such a thing in the house of her sister.

In the beginning I wanted to be a dutiful wife. I wanted to be an admirable wife. I thought it only fair to give something in exchange for the comforts. What a poor fool. A poor foolish girl from the other side of the Channel. I never understood why Edward had to go to France to find a wife. Does he find French women more appealing?

What will happen? They can't go on forever. They can't continue it. Sooner or later Edward will tire of her. Or her of him. The titillation will be gone.

I will not be a prisoner here. I will not allow it. She wants to rule here, but I will not allow it. One must never surrender to the obvious. I will not allow them to disturb the balance of things. One must control one's destiny. I hate the smugness in her eyes. I hate Edward's pompous face. How cheap it is. How awfully, awfully cheap.

* * *

I am sipping sherry in Walter Bramsby's sitting room. He wears a checked sack suit and a high turned-down collar. He looks uncertain. He always looks uncertain when we're together. As if he can't believe that I'm actually sitting here in his flat. All these silly seascapes on the walls. I don't understand what men like about the sea. I think the paintings are ugly. His flat is ugly. So much like his checked suit. Each time I visit him, I'm appalled at the ugliness. He looks at me with such pleading. Does he remember everything? Does he have a full remembrance of all the things we've done together? His maids are not at all appealing. One can tell a man's taste by the maids he chooses to serve in his house.

Walter is always so embarrassed when I talk of Julie. He does not like to talk of Julie when he's with me. He behaves as though he and Julie are already married. How spoiled he is. A spoiled English boy full grown to a spoiled English gentleman. Does he think me depraved?

"Are you unhappy, Walter?"

"Unhappy?"

"Do you find yourself uncomfortable when I'm here?"

"No, I don't think so."

"Well, you shouldn't, darling. Julie won't ever know. Not unless you tell her, of course, and I hope you won't do that."

"Certainly not."

"Then you have no reason to be unhappy."

"It's a bit awkward."

"Unexpected."

"Yes, unexpected. I never imagined it."

"And now you can. Now there's much more than imagining, isn't there? If you don't like it, I shan't come here any more."

"Claire, please . . ."

"Shall I stop visiting you here?"

"I don't want you to stop."

"I don't detect much conviction in your tone."

"You won't stop, will you?"

"You haven't kissed me."

He comes to me. He sits beside me and presses his lips against mine. A long kiss. I plead for breath. I glance down at the front of his trousers. His ugly checked suit. How brazen I am.

"Claire, darling . . ."

"Darling, I must see it."

His fingers fumble with his buttons. Then his knob is exposed. His pink blushing knob. Men are so much like boys when they show it. They want to be cuddled. They want to be fondled. One must make the appropriate sounds of admiration. I hold him in my hand. I stroke him with my fingers.

He groans. "Good Lord, be careful."

"How lovely."

He has such excitement in his eyes. He watches

my fingers. His eyes watch the stroking. I like to see the passion in a man's eyes. The room is much too warm. This ugly room adorned with seascapes on the walls. I finally withdraw my hand. He groans and goes to his knees. He leans his face against my knees. Then he slides lower down. He kisses my shoes. He pushes at my skirt and kisses my ankles. His lips pressing against the silk of my stockings. Then he pushes at my skirt again. I must hold my skirt at my knees while he kisses my legs.

"Walter, I think you have something naughty in mind. You do, don't you?"

"Yes."

The heat shows in his face as I open my thighs. He pushes his nose against my drawers. How he sniffs at me. He wants my bijou. I adore it. I adore the lust when they do it. Walter has such a ravenous mouth. I thought I would swoon last time. He lingers. Now he pulls at my drawers. He wants my nest revealed. He wants my furrow exposed. His hands are hasty. Then the silk is down and he's at me again. He burrows. He feasts upon me. I close my thighs against his head. I shudder at the working of his tongue. He mumbles something. My darling, he says. I feel his breath. I feel his nose and tongue. How intoxicating. Like the last time, I'm completely drenched. We have our intimacy now. He knows my drenching.

"Enough, darling, that's really enough. Now please stand up. Yes, that's better. Oh dear, look at him. I must kiss him. Just one little kiss. He's so warm, isn't he? Warm and smooth. Really, darling, you have a nice one. Impressive, I should say."

Later I undress in his bedroom. Walter stands in his dressing gown and watches me. The walls in his bedroom are covered with watercolors of country houses. I don't know why. In truth I find him strange. Seascapes in the sitting room and country houses in the bedroom. When I'm naked, he kisses me. He kisses my breasts. He kneels to kiss my belly. Then I pull away and I climb onto the bed. He kisses my belly again. He murmurs into my belly. I don't understand any of it. Adultery is such a silly thing. So completely childish.

Finally Walter drops his dressing gown. He shows his pale white body, his tool upright, his balls heavy in their purse. How impatient he is. He climbs over me and I raise my legs. He holds my legs upon his shoulders. His knob pushes at me, pushes in, pushes further. I think of Edward. I think of Julie. My sister and Edward. Edward and my sister. Then I think of Julie and Walter. Will she marry him? He's quite capable. He knows how to thrust. I squirm. I return his pumping. I feel his cods. His face is bloated. He makes noises. A grunt of passion in his throat. His tool sliding in and out of my sheath. Then suddenly he withdraws. He says he wants me on my belly. "Would you, darling?"

I smile at his wet root. One never knows who to smile at, the man or his tool. How surprising he is. His unexpected lewdness. I arrange myself upon my knees, my rump presented, my sex exposed. Yes, I want it. I want to give him more than I give Edward. That's the purpose of it, isn't it? One gives to the lover what one does not give to the husband. Walter clasps me. He fondles me. He squeezes my bottom. Then his tool is in my sex. He groans as he enters. He holds my breasts as he pushes inside. He begins thrusting. I like it. I like the lewdness of it. I wiggle against his pushing. I find his cods with my fingers.

I do like it. Holding Walter's balls in my hand as he does it. Not as much here as Edward. But quite firm. Quite pleasant to hold. Quite nice to think of

Edward while I hold another man's balls. And what does Walter think of? A triumph, I suppose, a great triumph. In my own case, a small triumph. And Julie? I'm sure she quivers in her triumph when she has Edward in her arms.

Walter sputters again. Sputtering and grunting. Men are so much like animals. Then he pummels me as he spends. He cries out in his spending. I hold his balls as he spends. I hold his balls as he shudders against my bottom.

* * *

I am not the scheming one. It was Julie who was always at it. She always schemed to get her dolls. How clever she was. She always had Mother's approval. She had Mother's approval and Father's love. She was the favorite of all our uncles and aunts. I do remember. I suppose she thinks I don't, but I do remember. I did hate her. I do hate her. The present is merely an extension of the past, isn't it? How we competed for the low stool before the fireplace in the drawing room. I remember the dark bronze andirons. I remember the smell of rain in the house. The old engravings on the walls. The painting of Joan of Arc. I wanted to be a king's daughter. I wanted pretty dresses. Julie always schemed to get the prettiest dress, the prettiest ribbon. We shared a small room. The old servant would stand there wagging her finger at us. In the evening Julie and I knelt beside each other to say our prayers. Two sisters. Our Father Who art in heaven. And forgive us our sins. And hail Mary. The log cracking once again in the fireplace.

She did scheme to get John. In the beginning she never thought much of John. She told me she thought he was a mediocre prospect. She said she thought she could do much better. She wanted someone as substantial as Edward. Someone with a large estate. Of course she never said that what she wanted was someone with as much money as Edward. What she did was point out John's faults. She talked about his faults constantly. In the beginning she said she couldn't imagine being his wife. Then somehow she gradually changed. I chided her for it. I teased her. I told her she ought to be ashamed to be so fickle. I wanted her to marry John. I did not want her to have a husband as substantial as Edward. As dull but not as substantial. Edward in his idleness. But John wasn't idle at all. John liked to do things. He was so grateful to me when I was kind to him. Julie showed nothing but ingratitude. It was John who bore the brunt of things. He talked about his highland ancestors. Julie would mock his pride and say he was hardly English. It was absurd, of course. John's family had lived in London a hundred years. Julie would laugh and say she didn't care one way or the other about John's ancestors. The truth was that she did not care for John. She wanted a husband and she decided it would be convenient to marry John. He smiled at her. He thought she knew nothing about the world outside. He hoped she would change. She had him bewitched the way she had Mother and Father bewitched. And the uncles and aunts.

Then one day they were finally betrothed and Julie told me she did love him. She insisted it was true and I must say I came to believe her. They were a handsome pair of lovers. He continually sent her white flowers. They would glance at each other and smile whenever we all dined together. Edward and I went to Paris for the wedding. Julie wore a billowing white gown. Mother had arranged everything, of course, all the details, the ceremony, a

Gregorian mass, mountains of lilies. I thought my own ceremony was more impressive. I thought Julie looked too happy.

I was content that Edward's income was larger than John's. With all her scheming, Julie's house in London would not be as large as mine.

They went to Switzerland for a brief honeymoon. Then after that they came to stay with us at Edward's manor house in Surrey. We had champagne in the evenings. Julie and John smiling at each other. I imagined them together. One sees the glances of newly married lovers and imagines them together.

I came upon them one day in the wood near the house in Surrey. I'd gone riding alone, and then walking in the shadows of the wood, and then suddenly I heard them and I crept towards them as a lark.

Secret spying. How amusing it was. I heard them laughing. Two lovers on the grass in a small clearing. I watched him kiss her. I watched him fondle her breasts. This was first time I'd seen my sister in the arms of a man. In the midst of passion. One could see the passion in it. Their passion. I was envious of their frolic. Julie kissing him. Julie lying upon him. Julie's hand at the front of his trousers. Then his tool appeared. They giggled at each other like children. She fondled him. She stroked him. I adored watching it. The way she toyed with him. The sun blazed down a the small clearing. She toyed with his penis in the summer heat. Then she leaned over him and kissed it. Her lips at the tip. Her mouth kissing and licking his pink tool. Her fingers stroking him. Then her mouth closing over the knob. John's head was now back, his face hidden by the grass. She held his tool with her lips. She sucked his root. One could see the gluttony in the sucking. I was amazed at her skill, amazed at her enjoyment of it. I stood there spellbound, watching my sister's head move up and down. And John groaning as she did it. The only sounds the sounds of birds and insects and John's groaning. The only movement the movement of Julie's bobbing head as she sucked his tool.

Then she freed him. They whispered at each other. Julie climbed over him. She raised her skirt and mounted him. For an instant I saw the joining. I saw the way she took him. I watched her ride him. Now the joining was hidden and all one could see was the way she moved upon him. She made throaty sounds. She rocked back and forth.

I was envious of their happiness. I was envious of the way he held her. I watched their spending. The crying out. The shuddering as he spurted. I watched my sister shuddering.

Chapter Eleven

SHORTLY AFTER OUR MARRIAGE, Edward and I travelled to take the waters in Baden-Baden. We had rooms in one of the large hotels near the casino. In the mornings we walked in the gardens. In the afternoon we took tea on the terrace. We listened to the birds. We listened to the muted voices of the guests. The liveried servants moved about with a quiet dignity. One had the feeling the servants, the guests, the birds, had been as they were since the beginning of time.

One evening in the dining room, we met Baron Albert von Broda and his wife, Helga. They were Prussian. They had come down from Hanover to take the baths. They seemed delighted to chat with us. Over the course of the next few days, the four of us became quite friendly. We walked together in the gardens. Helga and I would talk about flowers and clothes, while the two men walked behind us smoking their cigars. We never took the baths together, but in the evening we often dined together at the same table.

The Baron was very cordial. He seemed impressed with me and I was pleased. The four of us passed a great deal of time talking. Edward liked to tease Albert about the German adventures in Africa. Albert always remained benign. He had such red cheeks. His eyes sparkled with amusement as we sipped our wine. He said he and Helga had been taking the waters in Baden-Baden for years. He said they always returned to Hanover completely rejuvenated. "Healthy and strong," he said. "It's pleasant to be healthy and strong."

In our rooms, Edward told me how pleased he was that we had the company of the Baron and the

Baroness. "Capital people, aren't they?"

I said I wasn't that fond of the Baron. "I don't find him appealing. I think he's too Prussian."

"Oh yes, he's quite Prussian, isn't he? And the Baroness. They do make a pair, don't they? But you don't find them tedious?"

"Not at all. No, not that. Just a bit too Prussian."

But as the days passed, I came to be as comfortable with Albert and Helga as Edward seemed to be. We spent so many hours together. We talked, we had dinners together, we played cards almost every evening until it was time for bed.

One morning as we walked in the gardens, Helga began talking to me about her life with Albert. She talked of her marriage, her difficulties with his family. The men were far behind us and could hear nothing. I was surprised as Helga's confidences became more and more intimate. She finally revealed that for years she'd had a series of lovers. She said she preferred men of the lower classes. "One has them and that's the end of it. The best are the grooms. I suppose it's the horses. I suppose they learn something. Or perhaps they go to the horses because of what they are."

"What they are?"

"Larger in the parts." She giggled when she saw me blush. She was a buxom woman and when she giggled her bosom trembled. "One wouldn't think it was true, but it is. Larger in the parts and better in the accomplishment. The best boys I've had have been the grooms. Sturdy boys. Don't you adore the study ones? Yes you do, I can tell. It's difficult to hide things from another woman, isn't it? I do have the best. One wants them healthy and well-furnished. Large in the stones and thick in the yard, isn't that it? Oh my yes. You do agree, don't you?"

I had no idea what to say. "Yes, I think so."

I was grateful that after that we talked about flowers again. I did not want to think about grooms. I preferred to think about less disturbing things. I decided Helga had been teasing me. I couldn't imagine her with one of her sturdy boys. I couldn't imagine it and I thought all of it was a way to mock me. They were Prussians, after all. I was certain that in Hanover Helga thought about nothing but her gowns and her next ball.

Then in the evening, when we were finally alone, Edward told me that Albert was infatuated with me.

I was amused. "Infatuated?"

"That's precisely the expression he used. Quite infatuated."

"Oh dear."

"You sound dismayed."

"I'm not dismayed. I think it's completely silly."

"Do you find him silly?"

"I find him dull and pompous."

"You might consider changing your view of him."

"But, darling, I can't."

"I think you ought to."

Then he said he wanted me to encourage Albert. He said he found Helga intriguing, and that if I encouraged Albert it would be of great help to him with Helga.

"Edward, I don't understand."

He smiled. "I want Helga, don't you see? I think it would be most suitable if Albert had you in exchange."

I was shocked. "That's impossible."

"It's not impossible at all. It's an amusement, darling. It's quite common here. Quite ordinary, I should say. You aren't so innocent that you think it isn't ordinary."

I was confused. I had never visited such a place

before. Illustrious people from all over Europe came to Baden-Baden to take the waters. Some of the women were extremely beautiful. The men all seemed fabulously rich. All the guests seemed completely self-assured and at ease. Was it possible that Edward was telling the truth? But I couldn't imagine myself in Albert's arms. I resisted the idea. I told Edward it wasn't possible. I could not bear the thought of it. I could not encourage Albert's advances.

Edward insisted. He said he was certain I would find the Baron amusing. He said I ought to be flattered that a man as important as Albert had such an interest in me. He said Albert's family was one of the most distinguished in Germany. And he did want his chance with Helga. He said I ought to think of it as something that would afford him a great pleasure. He soon had me in tears. I finally agreed. I was completely wretched. Edward soothed me. He brought out a small box and asked me to open it. A necklace. A gift he'd purchased in one of the local jewelry shops. He kissed my cheek as he fastened the necklace around my throat.

The next day during a moment when we were alone together, Albert asked me if he might show me a small war museum in a nearby town. "I'm certain that you'll find it delightful. Please accept. No, I insist that you accept. Helga finds all museums completely boring and we might convince your husband to remain behind and entertain her."

I agreed. It was all arranged by Edward, of course. The following morning the Baron and I waved goodbye to Helga and Edward at the hotel and climbed into a chauffeur-driven motor car.

The car was huge and quite luxurious. But still I felt uncomfortable beside Albert in the rear.. I thought of my promise to Edward. I watched the countryside roll by as Albert talked to me about the wines that grew in the district. He seemed so remarkably certain of everything. He seemed totally secure in his understanding of everything around him. Then after a while he raised my hand and kissed it. He kissed my palm and then my wrist. "I find you totally enchanting. You've conquered me. I offer you my complete devotion." He leaned against me and kissed my cheek. I resisted the impulse to push him away. I thought of my promise to Edward. Soon the Baron's mouth was upon my lips. He kissed me fervently. I was annoyed by the taste of tobacco. Edward never kissed me after he smoked. It was still morning, but the Baron had evidently smoked at least one cigar. I was more wretched than ever. I was a prisoner in a huge motor car with a man I found repulsive.

The kissing continued and soon Albert moved one of his hands to my breasts. He fondled me, murmuring as he kissed my lips. Then he dropped his hand and stroked my thighs. He pulled at my gown to lift it. No, I did not want it. I refused. Not in the car. I begged him not to force himself upon me in the motor car. The chauffeur seemed oblivious, but he had to be aware of what when on behind him. Albert was amused. He said I shouldn't imagine the chauffeur was anything but a servant.

"Pretend he doesn't exist."

"That's impossible."

But he pressed his kisses upon me again and I yielded to his mouth. Once more he pulled at my gown. He lifted it to expose my knees. He fondled my knees and then my thighs. He said the skin of my thighs was like the finest ivory. His kisses were so hot against my lips.

Then Albert's hand moved to the front of his trousers and I quivered as I watched him undo the buttons. I was mesmerized when his organ appeared. The knob of his tool was half-uncovered, a round knob with an almost cherry color. Albert whispered in my ear that I should suck it. I stared at it. I was helpless. I watched his fingers pull at his cowl to completely expose the tip. He was amused at my hesitation. He whispered at me again as he stroked his tool with his fingers. I finally relented. I did as he wished. I lowered my head into his lap, lowered my head to take his knob between my lips. Albert made a sound of pleasure. I sucked his tool while the motor car rolled on. Now I could see nothing but the tops of the trees as we passed. Albert's knob was like a warm fruit in my mouth. The actuality of it seemed impossible, but I had the proof between my lips. Albert stroked my face. His fingers traced the stretching of my mouth by his organ. "Like Aphrodite," he said. "You remind me of Aphrodite."

Finally we arrived at the museum. We adjusted our clothes. The chauffeur came around to open the door. The Baron climbed out first. He took my arm as I stepped out. He smiled at me and led me up the stone steps to the small building. The square seemed deserted, empty except for the large motor car and the chauffeur now standing beside it. I turned my back on the square as I walked with Albert to the door of the museum. I had the memory of his knob in my mouth, the taste of his throbbing flesh.

We passed an hour viewing the relics of German wars. Crossbows and cuirasses and ancient muskets. A long case filled with a variety of medals. Stuffed uniforms with all the brass buttons carefully polished. I was uneasy before an exhibit of pistols used in the war of 1870. Albert was so proud of his Prussian heritage. It seemed to amuse him that I was French. He said he doubted if any French person had ever set foot inside the place. "My father led a brigade at Sedan. He was a great favorite of von Moltke. Unfortunately, I myself have had no opportunity to demonstrate my patriotism. Are you disappointed, my darling? Would you rather I had the scars of battle to show you? I have nothing but a puny duelling scar." He traced the line of a small scar below his left cheekbone. I had not noticed it before. A thin white line. I quivered as I imagined his face cut by a foil.

"Albert, the room is so close."

The Baron chuckled as he led me away. "You're much too pretty for this place. You must forgive me."

I was happy that inside the museum the Baron behaved correctly. I was thankful for it. I could pretend that nothing had happened in the motor car. I could pretend that I'd made no promises to Edward about the Baron. I was grateful that Albert did not take advantage of our previous intimacy. The rooms in the museum were completely deserted. We found ourselves alone in a hall with a dozen suits of armor. The Baron talked about the history of his family. I could understand little of it. I was too frightened by the empty armor. I sighed with relief as we finally walked out of the museum and into the sunlight again.

After the museum, we had lunch at a nearby inn. Three servant girls with white aprons hovered over us. We drank a sweet wine and smiled at each other over the plates of fish and fruit. Albert did his utmost to be charming. I drank more and more of the wine. I hoped to be at ease and I hoped the wine would allow it. The day was so pleasant. After lunch we had our coffee in a small garden. The sky overhead was the clearest blue. I refused to think about the intimacy in the motor car. I refused to think about my promise to Edward. I enjoyed the admiring stares of the people around us. I could see the wonder in their eyes. A Prussian baron and a young Parisian woman. It seemed impossible to them. The servants whispered to each other in the shadows.

Then finally the lunch was finished and Albert escorted me inside the inn again. He led me to a room on one of the upper floors. I went with him in silence. Now there was no way to forget. I was apprehensive. Albert pushed the shutters open and marveled at the view of the countryside. "One can see the Staufenberg. Come look, darling." He pointed at the mountain in the distance. I trembled as his arm slipped around my waist. A flood of hatred suddenly welled in my chest. I repelled the memory of what had happened in the motor car. For a moment I closed my eyes. I wanted to blind myself to the room, to the presence of the Baron beside me.

Then I wondered what Edward was up to with Helga. He was with her, of course. I remembered the amusement in Edward's eyes as the Baron and I drove off from the steps of the hotel. I wondered how quickly Helga had fallen into his arms. Then I wondered what the Baron expected of me. He seemed so satisfied as he moved about the room. I remained at the window, gazing at the Staufenberg and feeling so completely miserable. I told myself I had already given myself to the Baron in the motor car. What did it matter what happened now? I had already yielded.

The Baron had more wine brought to the room. This time he insisted that we toast the occasion with crossed arms. I thought it so ludicrous. He was such a blustering fool. So stiff at times, and then at other times so silly. Then he kissed me. He kissed my lips.

He kissed my neck. I quivered in his arms as he whispered passionately in my ear. I did not resist when he began to undress me. I was helpless. The door was locked and bolted. We were alone. I had promised Edward. I thought of the servants downstairs. How fierce the whispering must be. The Baron and his French lady. Albert's fingers were not at all clumsy. He knew how to undress a woman. A pink flush came to his face at each revelation. He seemed crazed with excitement as my clothes fell away. My chemise, my drawers, my stockings. He soon had me completely naked. He kissed me again, enfolded me in his arms, pressed me against his waistcoat. He fondled my body. His fingers toyed with my nipples. He squeezed my bottom and tickled my nest.

"Perfect. Completely perfect. Such exquisite little breasts. Kiss me again, darling. I want to hold you in my arms."

Once more I was crushed against his chest. He rained kisses upon my face and neck. He seemed taken with my slenderness. He seemed amazed by the girlish look of my breasts. I was certainly different than Helga. He chuckled as he spoke of his wife. He said Helga had such large breasts. An abundance of breast and buttock. He seemed amused as he contemplated the difference. He said my nipples were a marvel. Like two arrows. He covered a breast with each hand and squeezed my nipples between his fingers. Then he made me turn so that he might embrace me from behind. He held one of my breasts with one hand and fondled my bottom with the other hand. Once again he compared me to the Baroness. This time it was my bottom that occupied his attention. He squeezed my flesh. He kissed my neck as he tickled my sex from the rear. I was overcome. I trembled under his caresses. He urged me to the bed, gently pushing me forward, his hand continually stroking my body, my breasts, my bottom, the furrow between my buttocks. I was completely helpless. I was completely in his power. He coaxed me to bend. He made me kneel on the bed to show my bottom. He said I was too lovely not to be looked at. Once again he mentioned Aphrodite.

"Oh yes. Oh yes, indeed. How fine you are. Like an angel. Such white skin. And the breasts so small. Not like the Baroness, eh? You don't mind me talking of Helga? Say you don't mind."

"I don't mind."

"Your breasts are like apples. We need to squeeze the apples a bit, don't we? I'm not hurting you, am I? And the bottom. Exquisite. And a bit of touching here. Albert has a good touch, eh?"

"Albert, please . . ."

"You do like me?"

"Yes."

"You're perfect. Perfect bottom. Full and yet not too full. One wants to have flesh in the bottom, no? Do you mind? Just a bit of stroking. Be patient with me, darling."

"I don't mind."

"I was charmed by you the first moment we met. I wanted to hold you like this. I wanted to look at you. Then I discovered you were French and that was the end of me. I adore French women. How unpatriotic of me. I ought to adore German women but I don't. It's the French I adore. What do you think of that? Do you find that amusing? Tell me the truth, darling. What do you think of me? How tiny you are here. The French call it the little rose, don't they? So tiny. But we'll manage it, won't we? God in Heaven, what a bottom. I must control myself. Albert, you must control yourself. Give me a moment, darling. Just a moment to undress. Stay just as you are, I beg you. The pose is perfect. What a joy it is to look at you."

I remained as I was. I had no opportunity to look at him. I heard him muttering behind me as he undressed. Then he was at me again. His hands stroked my bottom. He kissed me there, first each globe and then between. I trembled as he licked me. He tongued the little rose. His fingers tickled the lips of my sex. His tongue licked and probed as I knelt before him on the bed. I shivered at the feel of it. I could feel the wet sucking of his mouth. He seemed obsessed with my bottom. He continually muttered, stroking my buttocks and thighs, his face pushing at me, sounds of excitement emanating from his throat. I was revolted. His mouth was ravenous. I was helpless beneath the rain of sucking kisses. And the tickling of my sex. He made love to both places at once. His fingers played in one place and his tongue in the other. I heard sounds through the open window. A girl laughing in the distance. I wondered who it was that made her laugh. Were they gazing at the Staufenberg?

Finally the Baron removed his mouth. I could feel the wetness between my buttocks. Then I felt his tool pushing at my bottom-hole. I cried out. He soothed me. He pushed further. I prayed for deliverance. I begged him to stop. He continued pushing at me, coaxing me, stroking my bottom with his hands as he pushed forward. "My little darling . . . how lovely you are . . . from the first moment . . . so girlish . . . God in Heaven . . . and now the rose is breached . . ."

I felt his belly pushing against my bottom. He gripped my hips and began thrusting in my back passage. It was too much. He was too large. I was certain I would not survive it. Once again I begged him to stop, but it was useless. His thrusting continued. He made noises in his throat. His hands gripped my flesh. "So fine . . . exquisite, darling . . . you do like me, don't you? . . . now you're completely open to me . . . a marvel . . ."

I cried out again. I was certain the people at the inn could hear me. Were they snickering in the garden? I imagined their amusement as they sipped their wine and gazed up at the open window. How stupid of the Baron to leave the window open, the shutters pushed out. I was furious. I hated him. I hated Edward. It was Edward who had forced me to be at the mercy of the Baron.

"Albert, I beg you . . ."

"What, darling?"

"You must stop."

"But that's impossible now."

He persisted. He soothed me with words and caresses. He said surely I must feel the pleasure now. I wanted to die. I felt nothing but a great heat in my bowels. Then he was at the crisis, his thrusting more forceful. In a moment he spent, his hands gripping my bottom fiercely as he emptied himself.

"Darling Claire, what a wonder you are!"

I felt totally debased. I heard someone laughing again. I was certain they were laughing at me. Albert pulled away from me and I fell away on the bed. I heard him dressing. He said he would wait for me in the car. He said he would have a girl come to the room to assist me. I covered my face as I heard the door close.

Albert and I sat apart all during the return drive to the hotel in Baden-Baden. How strange it was. We were once again so formal with each other. The Prussian gentleman and the French wife of an Englishman. He made only passing comments about the countryside. I had the impression he was extremely careful not to touch me.

When we arrived at the hotel, Edward was waiting for us on the steps. He greeted us, he smiled at me, he took my arm. I learned Helga was not feeling well. Edward mumbled something about a headache, her apologies. Edward and Albert chatted about the news from the capitals. The Baron said he ought to have a look at Helga and he excused himself. He kissed my hand before he left. I avoided his eyes. I did not want to remember anything. When Edward asked if I'd like tea on the terrace, I quickly agreed.

Edward said nothing at all about my time with the Baron. He asked no more than a casual question about the war museum. We dined alone that evening. The next morning I learned that Albert and Helga had left Baden-Baden to return to Hanover. Edward and I continued taking the waters for another week and then we returned to London.

Chapter Twelve

Today after lunch Julie said her spirits have improved. "I won't be dismal."

"Of course not."

"I don't like people who continually fret." She turned the teacup and looked around the room. "Do I seem happier?"

"Yes, I think so."

She wore a light summer gown and her throat was bare. Her face had a pink glow. I thought the room was much too warm. I waved my fan.

Julie quivered. "But it's the future that concerns me."

"What do you mean?"

"Well, I can't live here forever."

"Yes, you can."

"I certainly cannot."

"Darling, I want you to stay with us always. Don't you want to?"

"Claire, I simply can't."

"But why not?"

"It's not fair. And I do want a house of my own. If only John hadn't gone down in that silly balloon. It's awful, isn't it? Being a widow is so ridiculous. I don't have anything. I ought to have something. Don't you think I ought to have something?" She waved a hand at me.

"You do have an income."

"It's a pittance."

"You shall stay here as long as you like."

"You and Edward have been perfect darlings."

"We do love you."

I couldn't help it. I had to imagine them together. Oh, how comical it is. Perfect darlings. Does she call him a perfect darling when she rides him? I wonder what she thinks when they do it. One can't help wondering. One can't help thinking of them together.

"What do you think of Walter?"

She looked at me. "What?"

"Walter Bramsby, darling. What do you think of him? Have you changed your mind? Do you find him more appealing these days?"

"I think he's a bore."

"Oh, you don't mean that."

"Men are . . . impossible."

"Useful at times. I should think he'd make a decent husband. He seems adequate, doesn't he? I mean he seems to have the proper attributes."

"What attributes?"

"Darling, he seems capable enough. He seems qualified to entertain a woman. More than qualified, I should think."

"Oh that."

"I don't know, of course. I'm sure you know, but I don't."

"I don't know anything about Walter."

"Darling, you can't mean . . ."

"Yes, I do mean. I don't know anything."

"Nothing at all?"

"Nothing important. If you must know, I haven't been close to a man since John. It's not nice of you to ask, but since you did, you now have the answer."

"I didn't ask."

"I think you did."

So there it is. She denies knowing anything about Walter. She denies that anything happened in that theater box. She denies whatever it is that goes on with Edward. Their secret meetings in his flat in Bedford Way. She denies everything. She claims to be a model of virtue.

"Indeed."

"What?"

"Julie, darling, I think you ought to consider marrying Walter Bramsby. He's quite suitable, you know. He has a decent income and he seems quite fond of you. I think you ought to consider it."

"I thought you said you wanted me to stay with you and Edward forever and ever."

"You do know what I mean."

"I do, I do. All right, I'll give Walter Bramsby my deliberate consideration."

"Shall we have more tea?"

I never know what fills her mind. Is she serious about Walter? I think of them together. The way she milked him in the theater box. Walter says she does it often. He says she likes to do that more than anything else. She tells him she likes to see the spurting. He says she drives him completely mad.

After that Julie and I talked about clothes. I said she ought to think about a new wardrobe. "The fashion changes so quickly now."

"I don't know what I want."

She looked down at her frock. She ran a hand over her bosom. I suppose Edward likes her fullness there. He likes the rounds, the flesh heaving. "I'll take you along to my dressmaker."

She smiled at me. "Oh, never mind that."

"Darling, you must. It's a pity you can't wear my clothes, but our measurements are too different. You have more bust."

"And more bottom."

"That too. Will you agree to come with me to Mrs. Childers?"

"Yes, if I must."

"A new wardrobe for the new season."

"I shan't be able to pay her until Christmas."

"Don't be silly, darling, Edward will pay. He's

certainly rich enough to afford to dress two women."

I found myself gazing at her throat, the soft hollow that sometimes pulses when she feels excitement. It was pulsing now. My sister has the loveliest complexion imaginable. How exquisite she is, how completely exquisite in that open summer gown.

Then Perkin brought a fresh pot of tea, and when the girl left, Julie said: "I should like to see her poked."

"Poked?"

"The maid. I should like to see her with a man."

I was speechless a moment. Then I laughed. "Darling, that's very naughty of you."

"I should like to see a man in her bottom. She has a nice one, don't you think?"

"You've never talked this way before."

"I don't know why."

"We shouldn't talk of the maids like that."

She made a face. "But why not? She's only a maid."

"It upsets them."

"She didn't hear me. Besides, we do things with them, don't we?"

"Yes, we do." I looked at her. "And what do you do?"

"Do?"

"What do you do with them?"

She blushed. "I do what one does." Then she smiled. "Or to put it more exactly, it's the maid who does what she does. I don't do much of anything."

"Is it nice?"

"I'd rather not talk about it. I don't think we ought to talk about it."

"She licks you, doesn't she?"

"Claire!"

I laughed. "Darling, there's no need to conceal it. I have her do the same, you know. I do like it."

"You said we oughtn't to talk about them. In any case, I won't admit to anything. I won't admit to anything at all."

I wondered about it. I wondered about what she actually did with the girls. All three. I know she's had each of them in her room. Is she ever tempted to kiss them? Selby is the prettiest. And the prettiest little bijou. Is my sister ever tempted?

She talked of Paris. "We ought to visit soon."

"Perhaps at Christmas."

"I don't like the crossing in winter."

"Then perhaps next spring."

"Mother's letters are so ridiculous."

"Do you think much about them?"

A bubbling laugh came to her lips. "One must always think about them."

"The other day I thought about the grange. That day you called me to the barn."

"I did not call you. On the contrary, it was you who called me."

"You always say that."

"Claire, it's true."

"Not quite, darling. I have the memory of it."

"I don't think you do. You never remember exactly. You always have it wrong."

"Wrong?"

"Where he was."

"In her bottom."

"In the other place."

"Oh dear."

"And it was your doing, Claire. I insist it was your doing."

Her face was hot. I could see it in the color. "That's not true and you know it, don't you, darling? I don't know why you pretend. I have a complete memory of it. I was in the garden when you called me. You made me climb up that horrid ladder. Then you pulled me to have a look at them. She was on her knees. She had her skirts thrown up and he was definitely in her bottom."

"It's all a lie!"

Her teacup rattled. She had such bitterness in her eyes. Her lips always swell when she's angry. She has such lovely lips.

* * *

Walter is so helpless. He sits beside me in a hansom in Mortimer Street. The carriage encounters a break in the road and he pouts. "Where are you taking me?"

"To Bloomsbury, darling."

"But where?"

"Does it really matter? I thought you were fond of my company."

"I like to be aware of my destination."

"Yes, of course you do." I pat his thigh. He has such marvelous thighs. I wonder if Julie is aware of them. Delicious.

He groans to protest when my hand finds the front of his trousers. "Claire, darling, not here."

"And why not? I think you like it. Yes, you do like it. I can feel the evidence. You like to be touched, don't you, darling? I'm surely not the first. Tell me about your other women. I imagine you've upset half the ladies in Mayfair."

"That's not true."

"Then not half, a third. These buttons are a nuisance, aren't they?"

"Claire, please . . ."

"Here we are. How sweet. Just peeping. I'll keep

it covered."

"Someone will see."

"Don't be such a dolt. This fellow in my hand has more sense than his master. Or is it the master in my hand, after all?"

"Where are we going?"

"We'll be there soon and then you'll have the answer."

"I don't understand you. I'm not sure I ever understand you."

"Walter, darling, it's not necessary to understand a woman. It's the woman who must understand the man. You do know that, don't you?"

"I don't know anything."

"Don't spend. I shall be very cross with you if you spend in my hand."

Then finally we arrive in Bedford Way. Walter's puzzlement shows in his face. We enter the small building. We climb the stairs to the flat. I open the door with my key. We enter the flat and I close the door behind us.

Walter pleads. "Whose flat is this?"

"It doesn't matter, does it? You ought to be quite happy to be here with me. Anyway, darling, it's not this flat but the one next door that counts."

"I don't understand."

"Yes, of course you don't. Kiss me, won't you?"

He kisses me. I press against him. I can feel his erection. How impatient he is. He quivers with anticipation. Now he understands the fact of my presence with him in this empty flat. Empty except for bits and pieces of furnishings. A jumble of things. I haven't had time. Walter kisses me again. Now he fondles me. He murmurs. He strokes my breasts through my gown. He holds my bottom.

"I must have you."

"You're a naughty boy."

"Claire, please . . ."

"Tell me what you want."

"I want to make love to you."

"With this?"

"Yes, with that."

"First a surprise."

"Surprise?"

"Yes, darling, a surprise. I've something to show you. In the bedroom. Come along now."

I lead him to the bedroom. I lead him to the wall separating this flat from the one adjacent to it. The slide. I move the wooden slide and a wide slit appears. A thin slit. A thin opening in the wall. A thin view into the view next door. I whisper at Walter. "Come have a look."

How unbending he is. He stands there in his Victorian obtuseness. He whispers back at me without stepping forward. "My God, what is it?"

"It's a peep-slit, darling. I've been told this place was once a house of unsavory reputation. You must look. If you don't come here at once, I shall never allow you to touch me again."

At last he comes forward. His face is hot. His eyes are so innocent. He stands beside me and peers with me through the slit.

Of course the scene is already begun. I know their doings. I know the schedules. Julie is already naked. She lies on the bed while Edward sits beside her. They talk of something. Their voices are low and the words are only a mumble.

Walter shudders. For a moment I fear for his health. He whispers. "Good Lord, it's Julie."

"Yes."

"And Edward."

"Most definitely Edward. Now don't say another word. We don't want them hearing us, do we?"

Walter shudders again. His eyes are now glued to

the slit, his head bent in the effort, his hands trembling against the papered wall.

Caught like a minnow. Walter is such a boy. I look at them again. Julie and Edward upon the bed. She lies on her side, her full breasts showing their weight. Edward leans over her and kisses her mouth. He touches one of her breasts, squeezes it with his hand. Then his hand leaves her breasts and slides over her belly to her nest. She smiles and opens her legs to him. How pretty she is. Edward strokes her. Walter and I can see everything. Edward's fingers inside. Julie closes her eyes as he strokes her. She squirms beneath his hand. I know the precise moment he touches her clitoris. I can see his fingers in her wet sex. And Walter can see. I touch Walter's trousers. I find his buttons. All of them undone. His tool comes out. His cods. His swollen apparatus fully displayed. I fondle him as I peer through the slit again. Walter trembles in my hand as I gaze at Edward and Julie. I hold Walter's balls in my hand as I gaze at my husband and my sister.

Edward lies upon his back now. Julie bends over him. Her breasts hang. She has him in her mouth. She has his penis between her lips. How hungry she is. How gluttonous she is as she sucks at his knob.

She teases him. She pulls her mouth away. She laughs. We can hear it. We can hear the laughter, the words.

"You shouldn't have kissed me yesterday."

Edward groans. "Where?"

"In the drawing room, silly. You kissed me in the drawing room and one of the maids almost noticed."

"Don't stop."

"My hand?"

"Yes."

Her fingers stroke his tool. He seems so totally taken with her, so totally helpless. She watches him. She looks at his face, then she looks at his penis in her hand. She laughs as she fondles his balls. She turns in her bending. Edward gazes at her bottom. Walter and I gaze at her bottom. My sister has a glorious bottom.

Then she unhands him. She stretches out beside him and raises her knees. "You're quite ready, darling."

Edward groans. "Yes."

He mounts her. Her thighs are raised and the joining is hidden. Her breasts jiggle as he moves. She tosses her legs. Walter and I have them in profile and all that one can see is Edward's muscular bottom pumping up and down. Then suddenly he pulls out and he mutters something at her. Julie laughs and rolls over onto her belly. She raises her body, kneels before him with her bottom lifted. He enters quickly. This time we see the sliding of it, his thick tool pushing inside her sex. She groans. She wiggles her bottom as he pokes her. I hold Walter's affair in my hand. I can see how Julie grips Edward. I can see the fat lips of my sister's quim as she grips my husband.

"Edward, darling . . ."

"It's lovely."

"You can finish in my bottom if you like."

He laughs. "Good Lord, yes!"

His tool is withdrawn. He holds it in his hand, points it at the new target. Julie makes a sound of pleasure as he pushes in. Her bottom-hole. With a steady sliding, Edward enters her bottom-hole. They both groan. Julie wiggles. Edward moves more forcefully. Walter gasps beside me. His crisis is upon him. How amusing. How helpless he is as he spends. My fingers working in the milking. Pity the papered wall. The curlicues in the paper are so awful to the eyes.

* * *

The first time anything happened with John we were at a large dinner party in a castle in Newbridge. Edward and I had gone up to Oxford to visit Julie and John, and then somehow we all moved on to become weekend guests of a certain Lady Masham. She was a dotty old thing with a great deal of money and a paucity of brains, but she did have a splendid estate and a fondness for happy weekends. After the first dinner, I walked with John in the gardens. This was the first chance I'd had to be completely alone with my sister's husband. I took his arm. I told him how nice it was to be away from all the chatter at dinner. "I don't like crowds."

He patted my hand. "Then you're not like Julie."

"She's the prettier one, isn't she?"

"What?"

"I said Julie is the prettier one."

"I find you just as pretty."

We flirted. His eyes were upon my bare shoulders. He stroked my arm. He seemed surprised that I did not discourage his touching me. I was amused at the way he insistently gazed at my breasts. "You find them interesting?"

"What?"

"My breasts. Of course these are so tiny compared to Julie's. Not at all substantial." I pulled at the front of my gown to show my nipples, to show the long points.

He flushed. "Good Lord, Claire . . ."

"You don't approve? I think my nipples, at least, are pretty."

He mumbled, "Exquisite."

"Kiss me."

"He kissed my lips. He pressed against me. I allowed my belly to rub against the front of his trousers. His excitement was apparent. A conquest. How easy it is when the moment is ripe.

When our lips parted, he touched the front of my gown. He found a nipple and pinched it through the silk. He found the other nipple and did the same. "Superb."

"You're my sister's husband."

"Yes."

A simple statement of fact. He seemed so capable. I was envious of Julie. I remembered the two of them frolicking in the wood in Surrey. I imagined him sailing in his balloon. How amusing it was to have him touch my nipples. My long points. Nature has awarded me a certain recompense for the lack of rondeur.

After that evening, John and I shared our little secret. In London again, I kept him at bay. He pressed for a rendezvous. One day when we were alone, he insisted it was impossible to wait. "You can't put me off any longer. I don't believe you want to. We must meet somewhere."

I teased him. "I thought you were a patient man."

"But a man at his limit."

At his limit, indeed. I imagined his limit. I pictured the length and breadth of it. I hadn't seen much of it in Surrey. One wants the knowledge, the touching, the weight of a man's balls upon one's fingers.

I agreed to a rendezvous. We met one afternoon in a teashop. We drove in a carriage in St. James's Park. He kissed me. "I think of you constantly."

I laughed. "Immoral thoughts."

"Quite immoral."

"We mustn't drive too long. I'm expected at home in a quarter hour."

"But I thought . . ."

"Today?"

"Lord, yes!"

"John, it's not possible."

"You put me in a frenzy."

How quaint he was. I kissed his cheek. I touched him. I touched the bulging of it. I had to see. He groaned as I undid his buttons. Too many buttons. His tool came out long and thick in my hand. Formidable. Then his balls. His hairy cods bulged out of the opening in his trousers. He gasped as I tickled his balls. The carriage was closed. No one on the walk could see us. The driver was oblivious.

John shuddered. "It's unreasonable."

"Unreasonable?"

"We ought to be in a room somewhere."

"Not this? Don't you like to be stroked? Yes, you do like it. Certainly His Eminence likes it. Look how strong he is."

Impressively strong. What a lovely thick tool. He groaned as I stroked him. I had such fun with it. The heat of it. His throbbing in my hand as I pulled the cowl back and forth over his knob. Then a firmer grip as I lengthened the stroking. He was sensible enough to offer his handkerchief. Then a moment later he made a noise in his throat. A yielding cry as he spouted. A cry of complete submission.

We met again briefly a week later, once again in a carriage. He said it was imperative that I go with him to a room he had. I refused. "Don't you love Julie?"

"I love Julie as much as you love Edward."

"Then it's obvious we can't go on with this."

"Claire, I'm desperate."

"I should think you'd have more sense. A man who sails in balloons ought to have more sense."

I finally agreed to the accomplishment of it. I agreed to meet him again in a private flat. Three days later we were alone in Belgrave Mews. He kissed me. He pressed his hands against my bottom.

"Don't be impetuous," I said.

"I must have you."

"I want something to drink."

He brought champagne. I dawdled. I teased him. I made him wait. I thought of that lovely tool so eager for it. My sister's husband. How strange to be alone with Julie's husband in a flat in Belgrave Mews.

At last I undressed for him. His eyes were feverish as he watched me. He wanted so much to have me. I stripped down to my stockings. "Well, there."

"Exquisite."

"You always say that."

"It's the word that defines you."

How gallant he was. I could not deny my own excitement. I could feel the tingling, the signs of expectation. "A gentleman oughtn't to remain dressed while a lady is undressed."

His clothes flew away in an instant. He came to me. He pressed against me and kissed my lips. He fondled my bottom. I held his balls in my hand. His tool throbbed against my belly. How impressive he was. I fondled him. I teased him. My conquest of him was complete. In a few moments he had me upon a chaise, his mouth pressed upon my sex. He burrowed. How ardent he was in his burrowing. His mouth sucking at my juices. Then he mounted me. My legs raised. His muscular body so demanding. So methodical in his lovemaking. One remembers the force of it, the frenzied insistence, the sliding tool. He moved quickly to the finish, thrusting at me, his chest heaving. I felt the wetness as he spurted. The very next day he sailed in his balloon and that was the last anyone saw of him. I don't think he shared Julie's bed in the interim. In fact, I'm quite certain of it.

Part Three: Edward

Chapter Thirteen

BIARRITZ THIS SEASON. In Biarritz I confront the essentials, the beach, the seagulls, the balmy air. And the memories. Oh yes, the memories. Oh dear yes. So close to Spain and the beginning of things. How extraordinary it is now, how extraordinary to come full circle. Madrid in its grace, the yellow dust of Madrid, that moment of majestic portent in a dusty railroad car. I had just sat down, just seated myself in a compartment on the train from Madrid to Paris. Suddenly the door burst open and a perspiring fellow with drooping eyes struggled forward with two large travelling-bags. I was the only one in the compartment, the only occupant. He apologized to me in broken Spanish. He closed the compartment door and began arranging himself on the bench across from where I sat. A moment later the train lurched and moved slowly out of the station. I'd expected to travel alone to Paris, but how it seemed I would have a companion.

Before long the gentleman introduced himself. He was French and his name was Fontan. Hector Fontan, he said. He seemed delighted to learn I was English and he immediately informed me he was an Anglophile. "I love the English," he said. He talked without stopping, his face occasionally twisting into a grimace peculiar to the French. I learned he was a moderately successful manufacturer of four-in-hands, now returning to his home in Paris from a business trip in Spain and Portugal. I judged him to be about forty-five years of age and suffering from an excess of nervous energy. He seemed incapable of remaining still for a moment. He either talked at great length about one thing or another or he fidgeted quietly in his seat as he prepared his next comment. I was dismayed. I was certain I would have no peace until I reached Paris. Not a moment of peace in the presence of M. Fontan.

No other passengers came to occupy the compartment. Fontan pressed his conversation upon me. I listened politely as he talked about his life. Eventually Fontan spoke of his family in Paris, his wife and two daughters. "My purpose, Mr. Ransom. My family is my purpose."

I was a thirty-five year old bachelor and all talk of family responsibilities thoroughly bored me. "Ah yes."

"Life is a struggle, isn't it? We men carry the burden of life on our shoulders."

"I suppose we do."

"The women depend upon us. The little darlings. One carries them and one needs them, eh?"

"Yes, I suppose so."

"I have three. A wife and two daughters. A heavy responsibility, I tell you. What do you think? Is it so easy to manage it? I assure you it isn't. Most certainly not easy. The women must be clothed, the wife must be provided for, the girls must be married. A man finds himself surrounded by obligations. Let me tell you in confidence that as much as I adore my family and home, these trips abroad have become necessary to my well-being. Do you find that surprising?"

"I think it's quite understandable."

He smiled. "But now it's time to be at home again, eh? I'm anxious for it. Anxious to see my wife and girls again. Especially the girls. Two beauties. And of course the wife. I always miss her too. I'm one of those men fortunate enough to have married a good woman. A loyal woman. Excellent in all respects." He waved a hand at me. "And I'm certain the girls will be the same with their husbands.

Excellent women. When they marry. The oldest is ready. My favorite. Quite beautiful. You mustn't think I exaggerate. I'll offer some evidence, monsieur. Just a few photographs. I always carry them with me." He extracted two small photographs from the inside of his coat and handed them to me. "You see? What do you think? Tell me what you think of my wife and girls."

I was surprised. The women were indeed beautiful. One photograph showed the mother with two small children. A woman with dark eyes, a heart-shaped face, sensuous lips. The other photograph apparently showed the girls as they were at present. Two beauties, indeed. The faces were striking. I told M. Fontan he was fortunate to have the affection of three beautiful women. He smiled as I returned the photographs to him. He chuckled as he replaced them in the pocket of his coat. "Are you married, monsieur?"

I said I was not. M. Fontan inclined his head and winked at me. He seemed amused. He looked at the countryside through the window and began talking about his travels in Spain.

We had dinner together in the dining car and the conversation continued. Fontan was always animated, always talking, his hands and lips moving. I told myself the man wasn't as boring as I'd feared. I told myself it was better to have a travelling companion than to travel alone. The trip to Paris, after all, would be long and tedious.

After dinner, Fontan revealed to me that his daughters were also Anglophiles. "It's my own doing, of course. They adore everything about England. They pine to make their first visit to London." He said his fondest hope was that his daughters would marry Englishmen. I was amused. The idea that a Frenchman might have such strong feelings for England was unknown to me.

When we returned to our compartment, we bantered about England and France. Fontan proved quite familiar with London. We played cards. Fontan brought a bottle of Spanish wine out of one of his travelling bags and I found the wine enjoyable. The long hours passed one after the other, a long day, a long night, then another long day and night. Finally at dawn one morning we were almost in Paris. Fontan asked about my plans. I said I had none. My expectation was that I would remain in Paris a week and then move on to London. I was in no hurry to return to England. It was the end of a long holiday for me and my travels had been completely enjoyable.

Fontan seemed pleased. He invited me to meet his family while I stayed in Paris. I accepted the invitation. I was intrigued by the beauty of the women. We talked about my hotel arrangements. Then Fontan had a sudden inspiration. "You must stay with us. What a clever idea. Yes, I insist. You must be our guest."

He said the Fontan house was small but they did have a guest room. He said it would be no inconvenience. He said that his family would be delighted to have me.

At first I was reluctant. The offer was extremely cordial, but I thought I needed the comfort provided by a hotel. I should have less freedom in a private home. But Fontan pressed me to accept his invitation. He talked of how his daughters would be so pleased to have an Englishman in the house. Once again I considered the beauty of the Fontan women. I finally agreed to go with Fontan directly to his house in Boulevard Houssmann.

And so my first meeting with the Fontan women occurred on the day M. Fontan and I arrived in

Paris. A fateful day. One never knows the really important days until they are long gone.

Madame Fontan looked exactly as she had in her photograph. Older by ten years or so, but the beauty was still there. The daughters were twenty and sixteen. The older was Claire and the younger one Julie. They were as beautiful as their mother. M. Fontan and his photographs had not lied. He had also been truthful about the liking of his daughters for England and Englishmen. I was quickly overwhelmed by the warm hospitality of the Fontan family. It wasn't something to be trifled with. Chance had thrust me into the bosom of a Parisian family and I told myself I had certain responsibilities as an ambassador. But of course I wasn't that naive about the business. Fontan had two marriageable daughters and I was yet unmarried and apparently with a decent income. I understood the situation perfectly. I told myself a few days in the Fontan house would be an intriguing diversion and nothing more. I had no intentions to marry a French woman. I could never imagine such a thing and the idea of it seemed ridiculous. It wasn't very clever of me. It's an amusement now, but I certainly wasn't the cleverest bachelor in England.

I found the guest room comfortable. The furnishings were ordinary. The Fontans were obviously not aristocrats, but there were signs of a former elegance in the house. Perhaps Fontan expected his daughters would restore the family's fortune. At the moment, the girl to be married off was Claire. She was slender and tall, with a haughty look that I found intriguing. The younger girl seemed more gay and vibrant. Two lovely girls. There were also two maids that shared a small room off the pantry. Five women in the small house with Fontan. I thought at times he must feel bedeviled. Did he rule the household? Or was it

Madame Fontan that ruled? I suspected it was Madame Fontan, the dark-eyed mother, the one with the sensuous mouth. She seemed in total possession of herself, confirmed and comfortable. Yes, it was Madame Fontan that ruled. She ordered the maids to put fresh flowers in my room. I was to be treated like an honored guest.

At dinner that first evening, Fontan talked of his travels in Spain and Portugal. There was also some discussion of a farm in Normandy that Fontan had recently inherited from his parents. Then I was questioned about my life in England. The fact that I was a marriageable bachelor was of obvious interest to Hector and Odette. The youngest girl blushed when Madame Fontan pointedly asked if I intended to marry soon. The older girl remained aloof. She said nothing. She seemed totally disinterested in me. If her manner belied her inner feelings, I had no way to know it.

After dinner we moved to the drawing room and continued talking. Fontan offered a cigar and I accepted. Once again I was charmed by the beauty of the women. Or was it the effects of the table wine? I decided there was something to be said for the sparkle of French women. The girls were animated as we discussed the differences between Shakespeare and Moliere. Fontan looked on with a smile. He seemed content with his family.

We had coffee and brandy. I hadn't had any female contact in some time, and before long I began to look at the Fontan women more closely. There is always something to look at. An ankle, the curve of a breast in a tight bodice, the smooth skin of a throat, the play of slender fingers as they turn a wine glass. I was amused because it was Madame Fontan who actually appealed to me more than the daughters. Her face and figure promised an abundance of passion. I envied Fontan such a wife. Then I told myself that appearances were often deceptive. Madame Fontan might indeed be cold. One never knows. One never knows a woman until a degree of intimacy occurs.

During the next few days, I was constantly in the presence of the family. They dined with me several times in the Odeon district as my guests. They seemed pleased. I suspected the restaurants were more lavish than those familiar to them. I bought presents for Madame Fontan and her two daughters, a necklace of pearls for each, and a new hat for each of the girls. The Fontans seemed delighted by it all. In the beginning the idea that I might be a suitor to one of the girls was nothing more than a game. After four days it was an idea I decided to consider seriously. Why not? I wanted a wife. I had always found French women sexually appealing. I had no family of my own, and here was a family that seemed eager to welcome me into its arms. Claire seemed more and more interested in looking upon me as a suitor. When Fontan spoke to me privately, I said yes, I would consider the possibility of marriage to Claire. He was quite happy. He insisted we drink a toast. He was so French. I had a sudden feeling that I'd gone completely mad.

He told Madame Fontan, of course. I could see it in her eyes that evening. I don't think Claire was told, or at least she showed no sign of it. Claire and I hadn't talked much at all. Whatever courtship there would be hadn't yet occurred. There was still a chance I would change my mind and return to England. Was this the explanation for subsequent events?

The next morning my breakfast was brought by Madame Fontan instead of one of the maids. She said something about the maids being at the market.

Claire and Julie had gone off with their father to visit Hector's sister in Saint-Denis.

Madame Fontan bustled about the room, opening the shutters, fussing with my breakfast tray. She asked if I would like her company while I had my morning tea. She seemed pleased when I accepted the offer. She seemed delighted. She sat on the edge of the bed and we talked about Paris. One can always talk about Paris. She was a true Parisian. She asked me to call her Odette. I said it was one of the more charming French names. Before long I realized we were flirting with each other. Madame Fontan and myself. It seemed impossible, but it was true. Her fingers occasionally touched my hand as she spoke. Her eyes were the eyes of a woman responding to a male presence. I was amused. Then the amusement changed to a definite excitement. It was Madame Fontan, after all, who had charmed me all along.

We talked about national customs. About French customs. Odette recited an amusing story about the custom of kissing a woman's hand. Her eyes danced as she talked. She touched my hand. I raised her hand to my lips and kissed it. She laughed. I continued holding her hand and kissed her wrist. The laughing stopped. A flush came to her face. When I pulled her towards me, she yielded completely.

One always wonders about things. Was I completing her intent or did she decide to yield only at that moment? We kissed. Odette pretended to be flustered. She pulled away. She muttered something. Then she leaned towards me and kissed my mouth again. When our lips finally parted, she helped me moved the breakfast tray to the far side of the bed. Then once again we kissed. This time I slipped a hand inside her dressing gown to fondle her large breasts. She made a sound of pleasure as I lifted the weight of a breast in my hand. I rubbed her firm nipples. She kissed me more forcefully. Her hand searched the sheet that covered me until she found what she wanted. The evidence of my arousal. She gripped it fiercely. Then her grip relaxed and she fondled it more casually. Her eyes were bright. She said she wanted to look and soon the sheet was thrown to the foot of the bed. Her fingers worked at the front of my pajamas. She knew precisely what she wanted. In a moment she had me exposed, cock and balls in the air, her eyes feasting.

I was in fierce erection. Odette's face flushed with excitement. she cooed over it, complimented my dimensions. "Oh, how nice. How swollen you are. What a nice one it is. And the eggs." She touched my balls, lifted them with her fingers. "You don't mind? I like to touch. Certain things must be touched. Well, you're vigorous, aren't you? When we first met, I said to myself now there's a vigorous man. And look how right I was." Her fingers moved to my shaft, squeezed it to test its firmness. "Such strength. He's impatient, isn't he? Like a soldier impatient to do battle. I want to stroke him a bit. Just like this. Really, it's like a cannon. The two balls are the wheels of the cannon mount, aren't they? It always makes me think of a cannon. I suppose you think I'm awful. Do you think I'm awful, Edward?"

"I think you're ravishing."

"A married woman . . ."

"Completely ravishing."

"And the mother of two daughters . . ."

"You have the most beautiful eyes."

"Tell me truthfully, what do you think of me?"

"I adore you."

"You're a darling." She smiled at my cock again. "And this is a darling, too. An apparatus, isn't it? Something made for procreation."

"And pleasure."

"Yes, for pleasure. You mustn't think badly of me. Do you really have an interest in Claire? Is it true?"

"Yes."

"How lovely. She's a lovely girl, isn't she? If there's a marriage, then I'll be your mother-in-law, won't I? Well, we aren't so many years apart you and I. I'm not an old woman yet. I can still appreciate a cannon like this. You do want it, don't you? Now that we've come this far? I suppose we ought to get on with it. Just a quick one, darling. It's terribly wrong, you know. Yielding to the Devil like this. Just a quick one."

After which she suddenly bent over to suck my knob. No more than a brief sucking. Her tongue rolled over the tip. I was quite overwhelmed. Upon awakening, I hadn't thought much of the prospects for the day. Now here was Madame Fontan busily sucking my root. She worked her sensuous mouth over the knob and stem. She fondled my balls. My flesh soon glistened with her saliva. She sucked lavishly. What a remarkable woman she was.

She finally pulled her mouth away from my organ and smiled at me. "Are you shocked, Edward?"

"I'm vanquished."

She laughed as her fingers played with my erection. "I like sucking a nice one like this."

When I begged her to show me her breasts, she laughed again and agreed. The dressing gown slipped from her shoulders and her heavy breasts were revealed. Full-blown. Each lovely gourd capped by a dark nipple. I took a breast in each hand. I toyed with them. I lifted her breasts and pressed them together. I caressed her thick nipples with my fingertips. Odette murmured and moved forward. She lifted her right breast with her hands and offered the nipple to my mouth. How delightful she was. I sucked her breasts one after the other until she complained I would make her swoon.

Finally she rose from the bed and removed her dressing gown. She stood naked before my eyes, heavy-breasted, her belly sloping, a thick forest of dark hair at the joining of her full thighs. She smiled at me and then lifted the breakfast tray to carry it to the dressing table. Her bottom was glorious, full and thrusting, a broad magnificent rump with a dimple above each buttock. What a divine creature she was. The mother of two grown daughters. A French beauty with flashing eyes and a face and body from one of Renoir's paintings.

I hurried to rid myself of my pajamas. I was anxious to make connection before I discovered I was in the midst of a dream, before she somehow vaporized in front of my eyes. But it was no dream. Odette smiled at me as I lay there waiting for her. She climbed onto the bed and kissed me. She fondled my swollen organ and gently squeezed my balls. Then she used her mouth again, briefly sucking my knob, wetting it completely with her saliva. After that she pulled away. She turned. Kneeling on the mattress, she bent over to completely expose her bottom. "In my rear, Edward."

At first I misunderstood. I thought she was asking if I liked her bottom. I was overwhelmed by the sight of her full-lipped sex from behind. She was quite hairy, the dark hair growing beyond her sex and into the crack between her buttocks. My senses were inflamed by the intimate view.

Then I realized what she wanted. I was to fill the smaller orifice. The dark ring. Her bottom-hole. She said it was too dangerous in the other place. She said in any case she had more liking for it in her bottom. She was quite matter-of-fact about it. She said my knob ought to be sufficiently lubricated by her saliva. If not I might try some of the fluid from her sex. She talked continually. I touched her sex, fingered it, probed between the lips. I did as she asked. I lubricated her bottom-hole with some of the liquor of her sex. Then I entered her. There was no difficulty at all, absolutely none. The road was obviously frequently travelled. She began moaning at once, moaning and shaking her hips like a wild woman. I was in a fever of excitement. I was ravished by her broad bottom. I stroked her hips as my organ pushed and pulled in her stretched rose. What a marvelous grip she had. Women without experience never have it. I was unable to go on. I wanted our connection to continue forever, but I was unable to go on. I spent a torrent in her bowels. She cooed and shuddered and cried out as I continued thrusting. A marvel. A total marvel of passion. I fell away from her with a final groan.

She came to hover over me. She smiled and kissed my lips. Then she donned her dressing gown and left the room.

As the door closed, I sat up on the bed in a daze. What did it all mean? I hadn't dreamt of an affair with Madame Fontan. What would happen now to the prospect of a marriage between myself and Claire?

The outcome was less catastrophic than I supposed. Things went on as before. My visit with the family continued. The allusions to a marriage to Claire continued. Madame Fontan behaved as if nothing had occurred between us. We had no further chance to be alone. Now I passed nearly all my time with Claire. We were usually chaperoned by Odette. I was struck by the irony of it. The memory of Madame Fontan kneeling on my bed constantly inflamed my mind.

I paid court to Claire. She seemed receptive.

When I asked her to be my wife, she replied she would consider the matter. It was understood that her parents had already agreed.

After a few more days, I left Paris and the Fontan household. I returned to London, to an English life. I passed many hours wondering about the future. Then after a fortnight a letter from Claire arrived. She accepted my proposal of marriage and assured me of her affections. I returned to Paris with a ring for Claire and our engagement was formally announced.

Claire seemed happy. The engagement was to last no more than two months. I bought presents for the family. I insisted upon paying for Claire's trousseau myself. M. Fontan was grateful. He seemed satisfied that he'd succeeded in making a good match for his daughter. Claire would marry an English gentleman with a comfortable income.

And my own satisfaction? I think I was in something of a daze. During the engagement, I established myself in a small hotel near the Place Vendome. I thought of renewing my liaison with Madame Fontan, but she seemed to avoid any opportunity to be alone with me. I finally abandoned the idea. I concentrated on Claire. She seemed to bloom during the engagement. I realized how truly lovely she was. I was impatient to have her as my wife. The younger sister seemed envious of Claire. Claire said Julie was too young to understand anything.

Finally the day of the wedding arrived. We were married in a lovely church in Vincennes. The church was filled with the Fontan relatives and a score of my friends from London. Claire looked ravishing. I was amazed at how my life had changed as the result of a chance meeting in Madrid.

The ceremony ended. Outside the church I

embraced my new mother-in-law. As Madame Fontan's bosom pressed against my chest, I recalled the view of her bottom and sex as she knelt on the bed in the guest room in the Fontan house. The image produced a violent erection. I struggled with the front of my trousers as I settled down beside Claire in the motor car that would take us to the railroad station. Claire smiled. She kissed my cheek and told me how happy she was.

Chapter Fourteen

So now we were man and wife. Or not man and wife. We'd had nothing but a few chaste kisses in the midst of a crowd of Fontan relatives. Mostly Fontan. Odette's family was not in abundance. I was a fool, I suppose, a man with a fevered brain. I had married Claire, but I knew more of Claire's mother than I did of Claire. I was dazed by my actions, by what I had done. Did I really want a marriage? What had begun as an entertainment had now resolved itself into something else.

We had a long, dreary journey to Biarritz. My intention was to have a month there before embarking by ship for London. On the train, Claire resisted any possibility to consummate our union. She permitted nothing more than kisses and fumbling caresses. She allowed me to stroke her breasts and thighs. He small breasts made her seem so fragile. I discovered her skin was incredibly smooth and it pleased me. As the countryside rolled by, I passed the idle hours thinking more and more about her body. The idle thinking soon progressed to an obsession. Producing an obsession is always so easy for me.

On occasion Claire had such cleverness in her eyes when I fondled her. Was she a demi-vierge? I couldn't help thinking of Odette. If the mother was passionate, surely the daughter would be also. I wondered about Claire's girlhood; I wondered about other men, admirers who had kissed and fondled her. I sat there wondering as the wheels of the train clicked beneath our feet.

Of course I wanted more from her than just a few caresses. She pleaded for my patience. I must wait. My desire mounted.

And then at other moments I would consider how pleasant it was to suddenly have a wife, to be part of the great horde of men with we. I had changed my identity. Now I was an Englishman with a wife. How ironic it was to be heading south with her. I had met her father in Madrid and ridden north with him. Now I rode south with his daughter.

I did not look forward to Biarritz. I remember that very well now. I was quite happy to be with Claire, to have a honeymoon by the sea. But I knew Biarritz. I hated the shams of the rich. Claire said she wanted Biarritz because her father had always spoken of it when she was a child.

Then finally we arrived. We settled in at one of the larger hotels, in a room with a balcony overlooking the promenade. Claire seemed pleased by the place. She asked me if we would see the King in Biarritz. At dinner that evening she seemed fascinated by the other guests. Certain people in the dining room looked familiar to me, faces I had seen on the Embankment or at Prince's. I hoped I wouldn't meet any of my London acquaintances. I wanted a month alone with Claire. I wanted nothing else.

Then at last the day was done, our first day in Biarritz, and we were alone in our room. I expected now I should have her passion. I was eager for it. I wanted the ultimate possession. I wanted her naked in my arms. I had champagne brought to the room and we toasted our future. She seemed happy, her cheeks flushed. We kissed. I kissed her throat. She murmured something. A plea. A headache. A bout of fatigue after the long journey from Paris. I was dismayed. I kissed her with more fervor. She continued to resist. "Edward, I beg you . . ."

"I'm your husband."

"Darling, I know that."

"Let me undress you."

"Oh Edward . . ."

But she allowed it. I played the feverish lover. Thinking of it now, I suppose it might have been a ludicrous scene on the stage of the Adelphia. One watches the actors in some silly little farce and one thinks the doings on the stage impossible in real life. But the doings that evening, in that room in Biarritz, were real enough to make my body tremble.

I finally had her gown removed. I exposed her breasts. I hadn't seen them before. Like two little birds. The points of her nipples are long. I kissed her lips. Then I lowered my face to kiss her nipples. When I raised my face again, I found her expression was one of amusement. "Don't you find them too small?"

"Only enchanting."

"Enchanting?" She laughed. She glanced down at the front of my trousers. My enchantment was obvious. Her smile faded. What replaced it was not a blush, but a look of triumph.

I moved closer and made her touch it, the bulge of it. Her fingers remained limp, but she did not pull her hand away. Then her fingers moved. Discovering. Squeezing. I undid the buttons and exposed my root. She took it in her hand. She looked down at it, a quiet look, a look of estimation. At that moment I knew I was not the first. She had held other men like this. As if to confirm my suspicion, her fingers began to move. She was dexterous. A light fingering. A proper gripping. She knew how to milk a penis. With less than a dozen strokes she had me spurting. I groaned as I splattered her silk chemise. She seemed fascinated by it. Her eyes never left my tool. Her fingers continued to work with great precision, until finally she pulled her hand away and wiped it carefully against her side.

After that she pleaded fatigue again. She begged me not to force myself upon her. She said she thought she would be ill if I forced myself upon her. She said she wanted nothing except a peaceful sleep. Thinking of it now, I suppose this was the moment that I began to hate her.

* * *

We passed the next day in a tour of the port. We had a carriage drive by the gate of the Villa Mouriscot so that Claire could see where the Empress Eugenie entertained her lovers. I wanted the day to end quickly. I wanted Claire and myself to be once again isolated in our room. I did not care about the Empress Eugenie and her amusements. I had my own obsessions.

Obessions, yes. I was now obsessed with the idea of having Claire. I suppose some other men might have been more level-headed about it. Claire was young; the situation required patience on the part of the husband. The proper attitudes were well known to me. I told myself damn the proper attitudes. I sensed her resistance was due to something other than her youthful modesty. I was right, of course. I now have all the years to prove I was right.

That evening, the first scene threatened to repeat itself. Now I insisted. I undressed her again, this time completely. I held her slender body in my arms. I placed her upon the bed. I extinguished the lamp. I quickly stripped my clothes away. The marriage was consummated in a frenzy of excitement, Claire's legs over my shoulders, my tool pushing forward. She uttered a small cry as I entered her. But after that she remained limp, silent, waiting for the end of it. I withdrew at the crisis and spent copiously upon her belly. She said nothing. Then a low murmur escaped her throat as I touched her sex with my fingers. Yes, she would have that. I rubbed her conch with my hand. She remained immobile, unwilling to yield. She tried to hide her pleasure, but the signs of it were obvious.

* * *

Over the course of the next week, we had connection nearly every day. Claire finally admitted to taking pleasure in it. She was never active. On occasion she seemed almost bored. But the pleasure was there. I was experienced enough to know at least that much.

My irritation was constant. I expected the passion of Odette, but Claire seemed to have none of it. She seemed disinterested. She took her pleasure when she had it, but it was obviously not something she craved. Not at all. Or at least I was certain it was so.

She adored Biarritz. She enjoyed the trappings. Occasionally she showed a great envy of other women. She liked to stroll on the promenade with me. She liked to be admired. I recognized that she wanted to be seen as a rich woman. After a few days in Biarritz, she insisted upon a new wardrobe. There was not time to have any gowns made, but nearly everything else was obtainable in the local shops. Boxes and packages were constantly being delivered to our room at the hotel. I sometimes had the feeling that in marrying Claire I had acquired a prize bird. People did look at her. She received all sorts of admiring glances. She had an air of beauty about her.

Concerning my physical passion for her, she seemed to have no apparent involvement with it. Her interests were confined to the new life she would have in London: the house, the servants, the clothes she would wear, the London season. She seemed obsessed with clothes. Then one day in Biarritz she announced she was ashamed of her jewelry. She said all the other women had such beautiful things. She demanded a necklace. She said she hadn't a decent necklace to wear at dinner. I promised I would find something. Her demands were constant: a necklace, new gloves, would I think of finding a small dog somewhere? She said she'd always wanted a small dog. I refused to obtain the dog. I gave her the other things. My life had been completely altered. I tried to resist, but I found it impossible. I bought her a frightfully expensive necklace in Biarritz. She was obviously pleased, obviously eager for it. She showed a bit of warmth as she kissed me. Was there anything I wished in return? Only to have her again. She was amused. She fingered the necklace that now draped her throat. She turned to the bed. She knelt upon the bed and proceeded to uncover her bottom. Gown pulled up and drawers pulled down. Her sex like a furry little fig. My excitement was intense. I was to take her from behind. The first doing of it. My reward for the necklace. "Hurry, Edward, please hurry. I won't have time to dress for dinner."

The days in Biarritz continued, the strolls in the morning, the heat of the afternoon, the glitter of the evening. Claire loved the evenings best. She had a passion for money. She continually asked about the incomes of the people we saw. Did I think that couple had more than then thousand a year? She wanted to know the price of everything in the expensive shops. Towards people of lesser station she showed complete disdain. For the very rich she had a total awe. I decided it was greed. She wanted everything. I despised it. She had youth and beauty, but already I saw the avarice in her. She would never be content. I had this passion for her. I had come to adore making love to her. But my hatred for her increased. Hatred for Claire and hatred for myself. I had chosen her to be my wife, after all. Or had Fate chosen her for me? I thought often of Odette. I had the memory of Claire's mother in my room at the Fontan house. I thought of my former quiet life in London. When I returned to London with Claire, my life would set off on a new course. I was wary of it. I saw things that made me wary of it.

Finally the honeymoon in Biarritz ended. We boarded a steamer to London. We arrived in a week and we went directly to my house. It was a large house, a property in the family for more than a century. Claire seemed pleased by the size of it. She assumed immediate dominion of the house and I was thankful for it. Now all the tedious concerns would be in someone's else's hands. Of course the servants were quickly abused. Claire played the queen and required constant demonstrations of the obedience of her subjects. She showed a special harshness to the maids. She had them scurrying. She had them always busy. "They can't do anything right. The cook is always drinking. Yes, your cook. I've never known a cook that didn't drink. And the maids look at me too much. I don't like them looking."

"I hadn't noticed."

"They're not clean, are they?"

"Not clean?"

"It's laziness, of course. I think English maids are as lazy as those in Paris. They're all such greedy little things. Wretched and greedy. I shall find some decent girls for us. Edward, we do need decent maids in the house, don't we?"

She took obvious pleasure in the house, in her new domain. I hoped her attitudes would change. I told myself she needed to mature. I had a wife. I hoped the years of peace for me would begin. Claire did have intelligence. She had her beauty. I prayed she would find her soul in London.

But before long I understood nothing would change so easily. In London Claire's attitudes became more evident. She proved to be extravagant with money. She cared about nothing except her own pleasures. Soon after arriving in London, she devoted herself to acquiring the most fashionable clothes. Dressmakers were hired, then dismissed after a week. She finally found a woman in West Kensington who promised everything in a fortnight. An enormous sum was spent, hours of fittings, additions and subtractions and restitchings, and then at the end of it Claire was still less than satisfied.

She liked to amuse herself with her jewelry. She would pass hours at her dressing table, examining her jewelry, putting something on, taking it off, examining it again. She adored an evening out, especially the theater. In those years Claire loved the theater. But her interest was not the stage but the audience. What she wanted was the eyes of others upon herself. She wanted the people in the stalls looking up at her with admiration. An evening at the theater meant Claire as a queen in full regalia reigning in a box. The box preferably forward. One can't be seen too well in a rear box.

In the bedroom there was nothing but selfishness. Her only interest was the accomplishment of her own satisfaction. Our connections were severely limited in scope, quite unimaginative, always in her bedroom, always designed to afford her the maximum convenience. She enjoyed having my mouth upon her sex. She liked to lie on her bed completely immobile while I licked and sucked at her sex. She would never return the caress, not in those early years. On occasion she would allow me to have her from behind. This occurred only when she wanted something in return, a present, a promise, something new and invariably expensive. I always agreed. I would pay any price for the pleasure of holding her bottom in my hands as I stroked in and out of her sex. It was as simple as that. What a terrible clarity there is in one's life. When the fog is brushed away. I wanted Claire's marble buttocks turned up under my eyes. She knew it. She knew the power she had over me. She used her sex as a weapon to rule her little world.

Then one day as I walked in the hall outside her bedroom I heard a plaintive cry. The door was slightly ajar. I had a sudden fear that she'd taken ill. I moved quickly into the room. She was half-reclined upon her chaise. She wore one of her Japanese silk dressing gowns, the gown pulled open to show her legs. One of the maids knelt on the floor with her face between Claire's thighs. When Claire saw me, she kicked the maid away in a fury. The girl looked at me with horror and flew out of the room. I was startled, unable to compose myself. I told Claire of my distress. She shrugged, reached to a nearby table and found a cloth to polish her nails. "I don't know why you care. She's only a servant, isn't she? I mean they're not like ordinary people. Of course now you've made a scene and she's to be dismissed. Really, darling, it wasn't necessary to make a scene."

"I thought you were ill."

"Well, I'm not ill. In any case, she'll be gone tomorrow. She's a bit too cheeky. I don't like them when they're cheeky. My dressmaker says all the girls from Bristol are cheeky."

She forced me to agree the matter was of no consequence. I suppose I wanted to see it that way.

Her attitude was that I had discovered her minor amusements with servant girls. She said she'd always done it, always had them lick her when the fancy struck her. Then she turned coquettish. Did I like her Japanese robe? I hadn't known it was new. Things Japanese were so popular that year. The robe parted and her legs were exposed. She smiled as she noticed my eyes. She coaxed me, touched herself, told me how much she wanted me. She soon had me drugged. I refused to do it with her on the chaise. We moved to the bed. I kissed her thighs. I opened her sex with my tongue. She made a sound, the same sound I'd heard when I was out in the hall. A great shudder went through her as I licked her clitoris. Now there was no play at indifference. Now she allowed her pleasure to be displayed. I felt victorious. I sucked at the flower, sucked at the flowing nectar. She called my name as she quivered again.

* * *

In the beginning we visisted Claire's family in Paris at least twice a year. Claire always boasted to her family about the luxury of her life in London. The envy of the younger sister was always obvious. Hector seemed pleased by his daughter's success. On occasion he attempted to be paternal towards me, but I always refused the gesture. I had married his daughter, not his dreary bourgeois pretentions. Odette seemed at peace. Her concern now was Julie's marriage. She said they must find an Englishman for Julie. Did I find it possible to be of some assistance to them? Surely there were scores of suitable prospects in London. I found it all a bit crazy. I thought they ought to find a husband for a girl in Paris. This passion for the British seemed ridiculous. But I promised to help them. Julie was an attractive, lively girl and I said I thought there should be no difficulty finding her a suitable English husband.

In the Fontan house Claire refused to make love. She always refused. It became a cause of constant irritation, a constant bickering between us when we visited her family in Paris. She refused to yield. She talked of the prying of the maids. She talked of the eyes of her sister, the annoyance of her mother. Odette's annoyance. How stupid it was. But of course I could say nothing about Odette. I was caught in a tangle of absurdities. On one occasion I threated to leave Paris at once and return to London if Claire did not yield to me in our room in the Fontan house. She responded with a flurry of kisses, a touching of the insistent scoundrel between my legs. Amusement in her eyes as she milked me. I hated her more than ever. I was certain I ought to force her, but now I had no interest in it. Once desire is subdued, the mind returns to practicalities.

And of course there was her mother. We began again, Odette and I. Flirtation and feverish caresses. Oh, the hot excitement of it. In the Fontan house Odette and I always managed something. Brief, surreptitious but always something. Odette was sly, eager for it, never refusing. She delighted in having me spend between her lips. A hurried sucking of my root, my fingers rubbing her clitoris, while the other members of the family waited for us in a restaurant. Had Odette arranged it? I was never certain of anything in the Fontan house. Late one afternoon, we had a single brief poke, the only one in years. Odette knelt upon the bed as she had the first time when I arrived from Madrid. Now the bed was the bed I shared with her daughter, as her daughter's husband. Odette knelt with her skirts raised, her bottom exposed. That full bottom. The mother was so much more seasoned than the daughter.

Completely ripe. Her fig bulged with invitation. And above it the dark little rose winking between the broad white globes. As she had the first time, she insisted I use her bottom; she would not allow an entrance into the other place. She was in a great rush. But I was determined to take my time, determined to enjoy the moment completely. Odette rolled her hips as I went in. She was now past forty, in the fullest bloom a woman can attain. I found her appealing as always. I used my fingers to make her spend first, her rose-hole stretched by my tool. How passionate she was. I had a marvelous time with her. I was certain the maids could hear the noises we made. Odette's wailing. The servants had to know. When I finally spent in her bottom, she uttered a wild cry. She said she was ravished. She kissed my cheek and hurried away. I remember I lay upon the bed and wondered if Claire would ever be as passionate as her mother.

* * *

And then came Baden-Baden. An ideal summer; a physician's advice to take the waters. Claire now had more poise with the rich. After a few days we met the Baron von Broda and his wife Helga. Claire was delighted with them. She said they were all she thought the nobility ought to be. She said they were such an interesting couple. She insisted we spend more and more time with the Baron and Baroness. I agreed for Claire's sake, but I found them boring, the Baron pompous, the Baroness much too plump and much too sweet. I thought Helga was a woman of vapid sentimentality. But Claire adored to be seen with them and we were constantly together. Everyone in Baden-Baden seemed to know the von Brodas. I was amused at Claire's enthusiasm. The days were uneventful enough and I told myself one needed some amusement.

Then one day Claire told me of the Baron's attentions. "He calls me a goddess."

"Is that all?"

"Well, there's more, of course. Aren't you jealous?"

"Darling, I haven't heard any reason to be jealous."

"He wants to take me somewhere."

"Take you somewhere?"

"Yes, he wants to take me somewhere. He wants to be alone with me and I don't see why we shouldn't. You can amuse yourself with Helga. She does like you."

I disbelieved at first. I could not accept the actuality of it. But Claire insisted she was not joking. She said I ought to show some understanding of things. She said it was nothing but an entertainment, a dalliance with the Baron while I amused myself with the Baroness. She was certain I would find the Baroness quite passionate. She said the von Brodas had already agreed to it. She said she would never forgive me if I refused her.

Of course I was astonished. Then furious. Claire sought to mollify me. She said she wanted it so much. She called it a present. She wanted my agreement. She kissed me. She unbuttoned my tousers and fondled my root. Then suddenly she dropped to her knees and captured my knob between her lips. I was overwhelmed. She had always refused it before. But now she sucked my tool with great skill. At the moment of crisis, she removed her lips and milked me with her fingers. I was helpless. I spent in a great flood. I gushed like a fountain. I had to agree to the scheming with the von Brodas. I was convinced it was madness.

The next day Claire drove off with the Baron to visit a museum in a town twenty kilometers distant. I was left with the Baroness. I told myself I ought to make the best of it. The Baron had my wife; I would have the Baroness. She was not unintelligent. We had tea. I found my eyes drawn again and again to her large bust. She seemed amused by the situation. We talked of Europe, of the various spas, of the origins of various customs. Before long she took me to her room. She kissed me. She said I must wait while she undressed. I waited in the corridor. She finally called me and I went in.

The Baroness was quite methodical. She knew precisely what she wanted. I remember the pink dressing gown she wore. She sat in a chair near the open French window. When I was naked, she held my balls in her hand as she sucked my knob. She asked if I found her age distracting. She had to be past fifty. I answered as gallantly as I could. The fact was at the moment I didn't care. She was the Baron's wife. Her lips looked voluptuous as they spread over the thickness of my organ.

She was clever enough to stop sucking at the right moment. She talked frankly about what she wanted. I was to take her from the rear (she would bend over the chaise), but I was to withdraw before the end and spend between her breasts. Then she opened her silk robe and held her large breasts in her hands to show me the final target.

One recovers the moments, the isolated images. The Baroness naked, bending over the chaise, her milk-white rump, her strong thighs, a breeze from the open window. Then connection, my tool pushing between the plump lips of her sex, the hot gripping of her grotto, the warbling in her throat. She muttered something each time I thrust forward. I thought of Claire and the Baron. Did he find her clever? Did he find my wife clever in the accomplishment? I withdrew according to play, the Baroness turned, settled upon the chaise, called me forward to straddle her bosom. Her eyes shone as I spent between her large breasts. "Finish, it, darling, don't stop. There's more, isn't there? How nice." I think she was saddened by the Baron's escapades, but of course one never knows the reality of such things.

Later I went down to the steps of the hotel to wait for Claire and the Baron. That evening Claire seemed satisfied. We had dinner alone and nothing of any importance was said. I remember we talked about the wine. I thought Claire looked fatigued and I felt a sudden sympathy for her. For myself I felt only pity and bitterness.

Chapter Fifteen

I WAS A MEMBER OF A DREARY CLUB. One wet afternoon I sought refuge in a chair at my club, a chair beneath a lion's head. The lion, it was said, had been shot in East Africa. I sat with a glass of claret and imagined myself stalking a large beast across the bush country. Around me the men of the club talked of shares of West Indian plantations. I preferred Africa; I have always preferred Africa.

Then I heard them talking of something else. They talked of European nationalities. One fellow, a stranger to me, talked about the French. He said he would rather have a French wife than any other.

Perhaps some of the men in the group glanced at me. They may have been aware I had a French wife. I learned the man who had spoken was John Dallow, a balloonist well known in certain circles.

Later I introduced myself to Dallow. I reminded him of his comment concerning French wives. I said I had a French wife myself. He seemed pleased to make my acquaintance. I ordered another bottle of wine. I sat with Dallow in a corner. I talked of the Fontans and mentioned the availability of Julie. Dallow showed a degree of interest. We amused ourselves discussing the various capacities of women. "You might visit us in Paris. My wife and I will be there in a fortnight, and you might come by to pay the family a call."

Dallow smiled. "Oh yes. Marvelous idea. Yes, I think I'll do that. That's very good of you."

And so the next time Claire and I were in Paris, John Dallow came to call at the Fontan house. He met Julie. Two days later he came again, this time to sit with us at dinner. Hector was soon eager to have Dallow as a son-in-law. The three of us, Hector and

Dallow and myself, spent long hours smoking cigars. I remembered the journey with Hector from Madrid to Paris. I remember Hector's enthusiasm. Now Dallow received the entire effusion of Hector's passion for the English.

Dallow did not return to London; he remained in Paris. I suppose if Claire and I hadn't occupied the guest room in the Fontan house, Dallow might have been cajoled into occupying the room himself. And would the interlude with Odette repeat itself? The question pulled at me for days. I wanted Odette's comforts again, but this time she refused. The Fontans were too preoccupied with the prospect of having John Dallow as Julie's husband.

Julie was modest, unwilling to say much, but one could tell she found Dallow appealing. Before long John visited the Fontans nearly every day. One afternoon he told he approved of Julie. He told me he would proceed with matters. That evening, after Fontan had returned to his hotel, I announced the positive result to the family. They were all quite pleased. I felt a sense of accomplishment.

Dallow's courtship of Julie began soon after that. The pattern of my own courtship of Claire seemed to repeat itself in all the essentials.

After Claire and I returned to London, I did not see Dallow again for some time. We heard from the Fontans that Dallow had gone off to a meeting of balloonists in Budapest. He'd given Julie his promise to return to her in the spring. In February I found myself in Paris without Claire, on an errand for an acquaintance in Whitehall. As usual, I stayed at the Fontan house. With malice, I suppose, I decided to amuse myself with Julie, to seduce her if possible. I wanted revenge against Odette, against Claire, against Hector, against all of them. I felt a sudden wave of hatred for Dallow and his stupid ballooning. I told myself I would have Julie. I would have her sweetness, her ebullience. I made plans to remain in Paris until I succeeded.

The Fontans seemed pleased when Julie and I began to spend much time together. We visited museums, occupied tables at the popular cafes, strolled along the boulevards. I found her not at all like Claire. I became more and more intrigued. She would smile at me when I complimented her appearance. She seemed receptive to my advances. I kissed her in the Luxembourg Gardens. The kiss was returned. She pressed against me. When I suggested a hotel, she nodded. We hurried to a place in Rue de Vaugirard. A bright little room with a window overlooking the park. As soon as I closed the door, I took Julie into my arms again and kissed her. She pulled back a bit and smiled. "We mustn't, you know. You won't force me, will you?"

I answered with another kiss. My fingers worked at the buttons of her gown. "I must look at you."

She was amused at my frenzy. She remained passive as I undressed her. At last her breasts were revealed. Full gourds, a full ripeness, the nipples already swollen with excitement. She had Odette's skin, Odette's breasts. Her buttocks were superb. Full thighs tapering to graceful legs. Beneath her belly a dark bush of hair, the fur thick and prominent.

I fondled her breasts. They were so different from Claire's. Julie reminded me so much of Odette. I bent my head to suck her nipples. She adored it. She moaned at the feel of my lips at her breasts.

Then at last I made her lie at the edge of the bed. I opened her thighs, kissed her knees, her thighs, her nest, and finally her sex. She moaned softly as I probed with my tongue. She was still a virgin. Her liquor flowed in abundance. I nibbled at the plump lips of her sex. I sucked at the open flesh, at the bud of her clitoris. Her fur tickled my nose. I worked my tongue in her trench, reveling in the flood of thick syrup. Finally she spent. A groan, a shudder, her thighs pressing against my head.

"Edward, darling . . ."

"I won't hear any regrets."

She laughed, a soft, bubbling laugh. "I don't have any. But I do want the same. I want you in my mouth."

I quickly stripped my clothes away. She rose to sit at the edge of the bed. She smiled at my swollen state. She fondled my testicles, then my root. Yes, a demi-vierge. Like her sister. There was knowledge in the fondling. Clever fingers lifting my balls. Then her fruity lips opening to engulf my knob. A moment of unbelief. I had my root in the mouth of my wife's sister. First the mother, then Claire, and now Julie. Three Fontan women sucking at my penis. Julie's mouth was the most divine. Ardent but still fresh. Her eyes closed as she slid the ring of her lips back and forth along the length of my tool. Her fingers continued to squeeze my stones. I wondered what Dallow was doing at that moment. Sailing in one of his silly balloons? Before long I shuddered and spent in Julie's mouth.

We left the hotel after that. She would go to John Dallow a virgin. A month later Dallow and Julie were betrothed. Two months after that they were married in Vincennes in the same church in which Claire and I had taken our vows.

After the ceremony, Julie smiled at me. I gazed at her smiling mouth. I amused myself with the memory of that hotel in Rue Vaugirard.

* * *

A few months later the four of us were at my ancestral manor house in Surrey. John and Julie had taken up residence in London. We invited them to stay with us in Surrey during the month of September. The weather was mild, the days clear, the afternoons almost balmy. I thought Claire was sometimes unkind to Julie. Claire seemed pleased that John's income was not as large as my own. On occasion she belittled Julie's attempts to give an affluent impression. Julie would blush and remain silent. Did they hate each other? I thought they did. But then at other times a true sisterly affection between them was quite obvious. I did not know what to make of it. One never knows what to make of such things.

Then one afternoon, as we sat alone on the lawn, Claire told me I might watch John and Julie if I liked. "If you want to, darling. It can be done if you want to."

"Watch them? Watch them at what?"

Claire laughed. "Watch them together, of course. Watch him cover my sister."

"Where?"

"In the wood near the Jerrold farm. They go riding there. They have a spot in the wood where they do it and I've seen them at it twice. It's fun, really."

"Good Lord."

"Don't you want to?"

She coaxed me into joining her. Yes, I did want to see it. We had the horses saddled and we rode off. When we passed the Jerrold farm, Claire insisted we dismount and leave the horses. We crept through the tall grass towards the wood like a pair of poachers. I was amused, sweating in the heat. I'd finished an entire bottle of wine at lunch and now the sun made me dizzy. We soon passed their horses where they'd been left at a post. Claire led me along, cautioning me to step carefully inside the wood. Then finally we saw them in a small clearing. Julie was bent over a stump with her gown raised and John had already mounted her from the rear. He had his riding breeches down at his boots, his white rump moving as he slowly poked her.

Claire's excitement was intense. She trembled against me. I moved behind her and covered her breasts with my hands. She leaned against me as we watched them. She whispered at me. "He always takes her like that."

I raised Claire's dress to expose her bottom. She murmured a protest as I fondled her globes. But then she yielded. She bent forward. She used the trunk of the tree beside us to support herself. I found her grotto drenched. I penetrated quickly. A sound of pleasure came out of Claire's throat. The other's were too far to hear it. I pushed Claire's gown and chemise to her waist to completely expose her buttocks. I gazed down at the sliding of my tool in and out of her hairy cleft. My pleasure was keen. I was amused at my victory over John: first having Julie in Paris and now watching them together in Surrey. Claire squirmed as I poked her. She rolled her hips and whispered: "Hurry, darling."

I spent lavishly. It was glorious. And there in the clearing I could see John was also at the end of it. Almost a brotherly touch. How amusing it was to have the sisters at the same time and in the same way.

* * *

Ah yes, the amusement of it. And John's amusement? About a year later I saw them together in Tottenham Court Road. Claire and John. I remember the shock of it. She held his arm as they walked. I followed them. I watched them enter a small hotel. One of those places that make rooms available for an hour or two. My wife and my brother-in-law. Was I truly surprised? I hadn't thought Claire would be so daring with her sister's husband. Poor Edward. I have the misfortune of always being surprised by people. I walked down towards Oxford Street. Claire had long ceased to be an obsession. Now that I'd seen her with John, my hatred was fervent. The next day I visited the office of a private detective, a Mr. Cutter. I issued instructions to obtain evidence concerning Claire's doings in London. After a few weeks, Mr. Cutter provided a thorough report to me in person. Mrs. Ransom was certainly seeing Mr. Dallow surreptitiously and in circumstances leading one to believe the obvious. Tawdry little hotels in Bloomsbury. Mr. Cutter also reported that Mrs. Ransom was frequently in the home of an actress named Lily Graham. "A bit of a reputation, sir."

"Reputation?"

"She's one of those that likes the ladies."

Was there mockery in his eyes? I paid Mr. Cutter's bill and dismissed him. I went directly to my club and drank myself into a stupor. Around me in the club they were still talking of shares and plantations. Well, I couldn't blame John Dallow for Lily Graham, could I? The red wine soaked into my brain.

A few days later I found myself alone with Claire in the house and I cajoled her into bed. It was late afternoon, hardly the time when she appreciated my advances. But I persisted. I amused myself by thinking I'd upset a rendezvous somewhere. Claire seemed pliant as I fondled her thighs. I felt a mixture of desire and hatred. She granted my wish to look at her bottom. She posed on her bed with her gown at her waist and her buttocks naked. "Is that what you want?"

I kissed and fondled her bottom-cheeks. She purred with approval as I licked in the furrow. I tickled her rose-hole with my tongue. I sucked at it. I bathed in it a flood of saliva. Claire made sounds of pleasure as she moved her bottom against my face. She did not suspect my intention. Then I rose to mount her. The target beckoned to me. I first touched the lips of her sex to deflect her attention. I rubbed her clitoris and probed her sex with my fingers. Then I pushed my knob at the smaller hole. She was caught by surprise. She uttered a cry. She froze as I pushed in. "Edward, no!"

I pushed further. This was the first time, my first entry into a place I was certain had been breached by others. In the past she'd never allowed it to me. Now I ignored her pleading. She cried out but I showed no mercy. I thought of her with John. I imagined his tool stretching her bottom-hole. At last her cries ceased when she realized they were useless. She held still as I moved my root in and out of her fundament. I told her I had the impression she liked it. "You ought to be truthful."

"It's awful."

"I don't believe that."

"Go on, then. Please finish it."

I wondered what she did with Lily Graham. I squeezed her globes as I spent in her bottom. I drained myself in her rear portal.

I told Claire nothing of my knowledge of things. Now when I found her absent in the afternoon, I savored my secret awareness. I imagined her with John. Or with the actress Lily Graham. I made a point to accompany Claire to the theater one evening to see the Graham woman perform. I found Lily Graham charming enough. I thought she had a thin voice. Claire seemed quite taken with the performance, and on more than one occasion I thought the actress looked up at our box in a meaningful way. During the intermission Claire said she thought Lily Graham's performance was superb. "She's not well known, is she?"

I said I had no idea. "I certainly haven't seen her before."

"Well, she ought to be well known, shouldn't she? She's quite marvelous."

Our lives continued. We go on, don't we? The days pass and we go on.

The four of us, Claire and myself, Julie and John, saw each other in a group only occasionally. Claire remained unkind to Julie, snobbish in that way she was. Julie never blushed any more. She chose to ignore her sister's jibes.

John continued to pursue his obsession with balloons. He was well known at the club now. John Dallow, the balloonist. I avoided the club as always. I hated the place. I hated all the dull talk. Let them have their plantations and lion heads. I took to walking up and down the Strand when I wanted company. I suppose there were people in the road who thought me odd.

One afternoon I drove to Arkley Heath to watch John ascend in one of his balloons. He waved to me from the gondola. At that moment I had a premonition that John would soon be killed in one of his silly balloons. I realized I would feel no sorrow. I would feel nothing. He would go down in one of his silly balloons and I would feel nothing. It was true I'd never liked him. But one ought to feel something. I think now I hated him as much as I hated Claire.

In the meantime Claire had become more and more distant from me. I was fully aware of it. We hardly ever talked. We sat in silence through dinner, and then afterward I could seek the protection of the library. We had our evenings out, an occasional Mayfair party, a few dull hours in a box at a theater. She was away somewhere nearly every afternoon. I suspected she saw a great deal of John. Or that lesbian actress. We did connect with some regularity, usually Sunday evenings and Wednesday evenings. She grew accustomed to having me in her bedroom. She always yielded. She was unable to hide her pleasure in it. There was now a small jar of unguent kept within reach of the bed. Did she use the same with John? One always wonders about such things. I told myself I oughtn't to be bitter. I had my pleasure with her. She was more beautiful than ever now. Exquisitely beautiful. To see her bent upon her bed was incredibly exciting. I was vanquished by the marble smoothness of her buttocks, the pouting fig of her sex, the tiny brown eye of her bottom-hole. She always murmured when I applied the unguent with my fingers. I had the impression in those moments she imagined I was someone else. During the act itself she was quite silent. Except at the end. At the end she would begin a series of moaning sounds. This was always the pattern. The sounds increased in volume until the crisis occurred. When I had my root in her sex there were no sounds at all, only the shuddering at the finish. The differences between the two apertures were always predictable. I was certain that her bottom had been poked by others before my first entrance. One has an intuition about such things. I remembered the Baron von Broda. And I thought of course John must do it also. Sometimes I felt an intense jealousy. I was always very potent when I took her bottom and on occasion she complained of it. She said my thrusting was too strong. I suppose I did it in order to punish her. But I also suspected she favored the more vigorous exercises. The more I hated her, the more she seemed to enjoy the way I poked her.

Then one day John's long awaited voyage across the Channel began. We all went out to Arkley Heath to witness the ascent. John wore a bright red scarf around his neck. He tossed flowers at the crowd as the balloon rose. He waved at us, at Julie and Claire and myself. We waved back, Julie and Claire seemed happy. The balloon continued rising and slowly moved south until it became a speck in the distance. We talked about the weather as we motored back to London. Julie was certain John would have fair weather until he landed in France. Claire seemed lost in thought. Then Julie talked of a new play she'd seen and Claire visibly brightened when she heard Lily Graham was in the cast. I passed the time musing how these two French sisters had altered my life. Two days later we received the news that John had drowned in the Channel near Calais.

Chapter Sixteen

CLAIRE SUGGESTED that Julie live with us. I hesitated at first, but Claire insisted. She said she would not abandon Julie. "We're not savages, are we, Edward?"

I was uneasy about having the two sisters in the house. I thought there might be difficulties, bickerings, desperate intrigues. But Julie was irresistible and I agreed.

She came to us shortly after the tragedy, two trunks filled with clothes and a collection of mementos of her French childhood. I saw nothing much of John among the things she brought. Nothing much of anything, in fact; she had very little and brought even less. She was given a room next to Claire's and we began what one calls a communal life. I was surprised that Julie showed minimal horror at the tragedy that had befallen her husband. She seemed more concerned about the condition of her clothes. I often found the two sisters laughing at something as I entered the room. They never talked of John. The poor bloke was in the Channel somewhere and here we were comfortable in London.

I frequently found Julie staring at me. I wondered what she thought of me now. Her presence evoked memories. I remembered the intimacies. One always remembers the intimacies. Did she think of them also? Did she remember as I did? I desired her again. I could not help admiring her bust, her delicate wrists and ankles. I thought of the two of us together. Then I asked myself if it was only a way to avenge myself upon Claire. Perhaps it was.

As for Claire, the presence of Julie in the house seemed to produce an exhilaration in her. She seemed more energetic, more certain of herself. She was more demanding of me, more in need of my company in her bedroom. I thought she flirted with me more frequently. She wanted connection more often. She would smile and touch the front of my trousers at odd moments. During our bouts together, she enjoyed various antics previously refused. Now there seemed to be a compulsion to exhibit herself to me. She insisted I accord her certain pleasures. She cajoled me into paying homage to her sex and bottom. What feverish hours we passed! She teased me constantly, fondled me at every opportunity. We did a great deal of sucking, our bodies entwined upon her bed, our mouths working endlessly. I'd never known her to be so ravenous. Always with the lamps burning in the room. As if she wanted to be seen. She said she liked to watch me when I sucked her sex. I found her aggression exciting. I liked to look at her in the nude. I liked to look at her sex and she would always accommodate my interest. She called it her little fig. She would half recline upon the chaise, open her thighs and part the lips of her sex with her fingers to show me the pink interior. On occasion the pose was more blatant, Claire on the bed on her knees, her sex exposed to me from the rear. Then her sex did indeed resemble a fig, and when I told her so she seemed quite amused at my description of it. Then she would request my mouth and I would suck her like that, her body bent upon the bed, my tongue licking at her little fig from the rear. She moaned constantly whenever she felt the lapping of my tongue. And other poses, all the lecherous poses in her bedroom. I saw more of her body now than ever before. She constantly fondled me in her bedroom, held my testicles and root, teased me about my excitement, on occasion a compliment concerning my virility.

But my hatred for Claire did not diminish. I hated her even as I sucked her sex. My desire for her was always strong, but now I also wanted Julie. Claire's sister was in the house and always present in my mind. I wanted the complete possession of Julie. The past moments of intimacy between us had become burning memories.

I was also wary of Julie, wary of my desire for her. I told myself I was easily caught by a woman. An affair with Julie might be dangerous. Claire might discover it. I did not like complications. I wanted a simple life. Claire was so unpredictable. She knew everything that went on in the house. She knew all the details of my life. She would sense an affair with her sister. Or else Julie would reveal it. I would have an abominable intrigue in my house. Two French sisters whispering together in secret moments. I would find myself wary of shadows. I remembered the cloying atmosphere of the Fontan house in Paris. I envisioned myself transformed into one of those wretched men who occupy a wing-chair in an empty club, their eyes glassy as they hide their souls behind the pages of a newspaper. There would be twistings and turnings in the house, a tangle of deceptions.

Then at other times I found the idea of an affair with Julie amusing. What a lark to have two sisters. I had to admit my weakness for deceptions, my own deceptions. I did enjoy the games of intrigue. And I found Julie so exciting. The younger sister was so remarkably ripe. Like a fruit to be plucked again now that John was gone. What could be more convenient than her presence here in the house? She was so much more appealing than Claire, more like Odette. I could not forget Odette. I told myself I'd had the mother and one daughter and now I should have the other daughter as well. All the Fontan women. I should taste them all. A dalliance with Julie would be delicious. I passed fevered hours thinking about her. I wanted to hold her breasts, her bottom, the slope of her belly. I wanted her flesh in my hands. I wanted to suck at her fountain. I wanted the feel of her ripe sex beneath my fingers.

Then one day the affair with Julie finally began. Perhaps the accomplishment of it was inevitable.

We found each other alone in the house. We had tea together in the library. We flirted with each other and she seemed quite receptive. At last we kissed.

"Edward, we mustn't."

"Why not?"

"I don't know. It's not proper."

"I haven't forgotten you."

"I don't want to talk about that. I was much too young."

"Old enough, I think."

"You took advantage of me."

"Yes, I think I did. How awful of me."

I kissed her again. My tongue slipped between her lips as we pressed against each other. The memories of her body flooded my brain. I remembered her mouth on my penis, the ardent sucking. We kissed again and she touched me. She laughed as she pinched my root through my trousers. Now all the pretense of modesty vanished. She was a woman now, a young widow. She unbuttoned my trousers, brought my tool out to fondle it. She held it in her hand, looked down at it with a smile. Then she went to her knees upon the carpet. She looked up at me, smiling, teasing me with her smile. "You've corrupted me, darling. I'm completely corrupted, aren't I? What a lovely thing this is. So arrogant, isn't he?" And the next moment she took my knob between her lips. I felt her tongue rolling over the tip of my root. I looked down at her with great pleasure. My penis in the mouth of Claire's sister. She had such a lovely mouth, the lips full and obviously made for sucking. And lovely white teeth. I spent in her mouth. She took the jetting. She seemed eager for my spending. I watched her throat as she swallowed. What a marvelous thing it is to watch a woman who enjoys using her mouth. My excitement was keen and a shudder of pleasure went through me. She looked up at my face with glistening lips. "Well, it's done, isn't it? I'm sure I'll be sorry for it. You mustn't ever tell Claire. I'll never forgive you if you tell Claire. You must promise me, Edward. Do you promise?"

"Yes, I promise."

"Look how droopy he is now. Not so arrogant any more. Help me stand, will you? I don't know why I've done it, but I have, haven't I?"

She dabbed at her lips with a handkerchief. She glanced at the mirror to see the flush in her face. Then she turned again and smiled and asked me to call for more tea.

More than a week passed before Julie and I were alone again. In the interim her eyes seemed always amused when they met mine. We had our little secret now. Then finally one day we were together again. Claire was out and Julie and I had at least two hours to ourselves. This time we went directly to her bedroom. She seemed gay as she pulled the drapes closed. She quickly disrobed and I did the same. We lay naked together upon her bed. I fondled her breasts as I kissed her mouth. Then I knelt between her legs to kiss her sex. She laughed as she pulled her knees back to her breasts. Then she moaned as I began sucking her. What a lovely ripe sex she had. Her sounds of pleasure were constant as I licked and sucked and nibbled at her source. A delicious feast, her syrup plentiful, her flesh swollen and hot. I made her spend with my lips and tongue, my mouth pressed against her sex as she trembled and groaned. Then I made her roll over and raise her bottom. She smiled at me over her shoulders and asked if I found her beautiful. I paid homage to her bottom. I rained kisses over the globes. She was soon once again in a frenzy of arousal. She pressed her bottom against my face. "Darling, don't tease me. You're an awful man, you know. A bounder. That's the proper word, isn't it? My sister's husband. We must both be mad. Oh, do it there. I do like it. I like the tickling."

I tongued her rosette. Her little rose. The puckered ring of her rear portal. She groaned as I slipped my tongue inside. I fluttered my tongue as she moaned. She mumbled something about Claire again. At the moment I had no thought of Claire. The globes of Julie's bottom were so full in my hands. She moaned and shuddered under my kisses.

Then I pulled my face away. I stroked her sex with my fingers and set about to mount her. I first entered her sex, pushing in, beginning the sliding as she remained bent upon the bed. I fondled her breasts as I poked her source. After a dozen strokes, I pulled out and teased her with my fingers again. She turned wild, begged me to continue. Now I was in command of things. I left the bed to find some ointment. When I returned, I anointed her rose-hole. She remained bent, her hips raised, her body trembling as she waited. I tickled her sex again. Then I pushed my knob at her bottom-hole. She groaned. She adored it. She urged me on. Her bottom was so luscious, so round and fully fleshed. So much like Odette's. I fondled her globes as I slowly poked her bottom. After a while I spent and she cried out as she felt the jetting. She cried out and squeezed my root with her bottom-hole. "Edward, you've exhausted me."

I enjoyed the intensity of my lust. I felt reborn. How amusing to have thought of her mother while I poked her. Now there were no regrets. Julie's presence in the house was a complete delight. I would have a new obsession. That afternoon I thought we might linger, but Julie insisted she had too much fear of Claire's return. She pressed against me, came into my arms and kissed me. I ran my hands over her nether-cheeks, fondled her globes to remind her of our intimacy. "Edward, you're a cad."

"You called me a bounder."

"Don't touch me there."

"I've just poked it."

"It's not proper."

Following that afternoon, the affair between Julie and myself continued. Whenever Claire was absent, Julie and I rushed into each other's arms. My sister-in-law became my mistress. We had our whisperings. We had our secret glances in the drawing room. Before long I took her to the flat in Bedford Way. Now we had complete privacy. We would meet there two or three afternoons a week. Either Julie or myself would arrive first, and then a short time later we would be together. We had afternoons of frenzy, afternoons of casual caresses, afternoons of stolen pleasure. I discovered Julie to be a complete hedonist. She enjoyed teasing, but the teasing was different than with Claire. Julie was more a cocotte than Claire. She assumed poses to expose herself. I found her a vibrant mistress, a woman whose passion matched mine. The affair both amused and aroused me. I did enjoy the excitement of deception. The idea of deceiving Claire with her sister was pleasant. I felt as though I'd achieved a great victory. Was Julie also pleased? I found it difficult to tell. She refused to be serious about anything. She seemed to think of nothing but her pleasures, her wardrobe, the hat she would wear to the next performance at the Adelphia. "Edward, you don't understand these things. But of course you don't. And I'm certain Claire thinks the same as I do. Doesn't she? Oh, it's nasty, isn't it? We lie here together on this bed of sin. My sister's husband. I ought to be punished. What punishment would you have for me? Kiss me, darling. Yes, like that. How sweet you are. I've always been fond of you, haven't I? From that first moment when you arrived with Father from Spain."

The interludes in Bedford Way were always intense. We devoted ourselves to physical pleasure. I was constantly afraid Claire would notice the glow in Julie's face. I wondered when the intensity would fade, the affair begin its decline. One ought to expect a decline in things. Julie continued her involvement with Walter Bramsby even during her visits to the flat in Bedford Way. So both Walter Bramsby and Claire were deceived. On occasion I found myself jealous. I was annoyed at the hours Julie passed with Walter. But I controlled my jealousy. I told myself I had to be patient. As long as Julie continued to visit the flat in Bedford Way, I would accept Walter Bramsby. I would allow Walter his moments with Julie.

Julie did talk to me about Walter Bramsby. She told me she thought Walter was a child. She wanted my advice. What ought she to do with Walter? Did I think she ought to marry Bramsby? Did she need a husband? She hinted that if she did marry Walter, she would continue to come to the flat in Bedford Way. But I was not delighted with that prospect. The affair would become much too complicated. Julie talked and talked about Walter Bramsby. She talked about Walter while we lay in each other's arms. One time she talked about Walter while she licked and sucked my root. I watched her voluptuous mouth. I found it amusing. She was such a wanton. So much like her mother. And yet so unlike her sister. I considered the mysteries of inheritance, the passage of things from one generation to the next. Two Fontan sisters were now in London. Had the French conquered England or had the English conquered France? Was I the vanquished or the conqueror? I adored stroking her flesh. What a magnificent bottom she had. And her breasts. She liked to hover over me, her breasts suspended, her nipples teasing my lips. I would tickle her nest while I sucked her breasts. The room filled with her groaning. No more talk of Walter Bramsby as she mounted me, as I held her globes in my hands. Life becomes bearable during a minute or two of a woman rocking upon one's tool. Then the turning, the rolling over upon her belly. "Do my bottom, darling." She did want it. She liked to proffer it, her hips elevated to show the moons, the deep split between her cheeks, the hairy fig. I wondered if she deliberately behaved this way to put me in a frenzy. And of course she always succeeded. Vanquished or conqueror?

In the meantime I became suspicious that Claire had a steady lover again. I felt it in my bones. I watched her carefully at dinner. I took note of her absences. I found myself intensely curious about the adventures of my wife. I wondered who it could be. After a time my curiosity reached an unbearable intensity and I once more engaged Mr. Cutter.

One needs these people. They provide us with a degree of rectitude. The detective soon reported that my wife made frequent visits to the rooms of a gentleman named Walter Bramsby.

My shock quickly turned to amusement. I was delighted by the irony. It was all so delicious. I questioned Cutter about details. I wanted every detail. He told me of his spying upon Claire. How amusing it was. Now I felt the power I had over them.

Then Cutter informed me that Claire also often visited a house in Bedford Way.

Now I was taken aback. Now I was astounded. I questioned Cutter to make certain he was not mistaken. But of course he was certain of it. He described the street, the house, Claire's entrance and exit. Was I pale as I listened?

Later I made inquiries with the woman who owned the building in Bedford Way. I described Claire to her. Yes, she knew the woman. I was shown the flat next to mine. I trembled as I entered. I studied the wall that separated the two flats and in a moment I found the peep-slit. The house, after all, had once been a notorious bordello. I stood transfixed before the peep-slit. Now I understood that Claire came to Bedford Way to spy upon myself and Julie.

How absurd it was. Claire knew all about my affair with her sister. It was quite astonishing. I was completely stunned by it. If it hadn't been for Mr. Cutter, I would never have known it.

Then I was amused again. It was all so ridiculous. I decided I would play on. I would have my entertainments. I would not reveal to Claire that I knew anything. I would retain the power of my knowledge. No, I would not reveal myself yet. What a lovely tangle it was. I thought of Claire with Walter Bramsby. I could hardly imagine it and I wondered how they managed things. How did they get on? Sometimes I would sit in a trance as I wondered about it. Claire and Walter. Her secret afternoons. Heated interludes in Bramsby's rooms. He was such a dolt. What on earth did she do with him in bed? All her tricks? I pitied Bramsby. He was in the clutches of a Parisian witch. I imagined Claire showing her sex to him, her thighs apart as she pulled at her sex with her fingers to show her clitoris. Did he take her bottom? Claire and I hadn't had connection in weeks and I told myself I had to pay some attention to her attributes. I wanted signs. I wanted her sex swollen in my hand after an hour or two in secret with Walter Bramsby. Then I told myself I was a fool and that to want such a thing was madness. But of course it was all mad and the wanting of a madness was of no consequence.

How amusing it was that Walter Bramsby was actually cuckolding me. I wondered what he thought about that. Did he feel remorse?

When Julie and I were next in the flat in Bedford Way, I listened carefully for noises from the flat adjoining. My excitement was intense as I thought of Claire on the other side of that wall, Claire with her eyes at the peep-slit. Then I did hear something. Yes, there was something, someone in the adjacent flat. Claire was there at the peep-slit. I knew it. I found myself delighted as I played with Julie. I thought of Claire watching us as I fondled Julie's breasts. My caresses were deliberate. I produced a performance for the entertainment of my wife. I chided myself for being so devilish. I teased Julie into a state of extreme lewdness. Yes, let Claire see it. I wanted Claire to watch her sister. I cajoled Julie into fondling herself. She lay upon the bed completely wanton, her thighs apart, her fingers in her nest. She did enjoy exhibiting herself. She opened her sex to show me how wet she was. Did Claire see it also? I brought out the leather godemiche I always kept in the flat. Julie was delighted with it and immediately pushed it inside her grotto. She moaned as the dildo penetrated her sex. She lay there in a state of complete frenzy. "Oh Edward, it's lovely. What a monster it is! So big. Really, Edward, you ought to be jealous. Are you jealous, darling? Yes, you are. You do like watching me, don't you? I want you in my bottom afterward. We'll have such a lovely poke, won't we, darling?" I coaxed her. She groaned. She continued pushing and pulling at the leather instrument in her grotto. I was happy at her wanton behavior. I told her to go on with it. The idea that Claire was watching it was immensely exciting. I tried to imagine what Claire was feeling as she watched it. Was Claire shocked at Julie's behavior in Bedford Way?

Then one day in a carriage, I amused myself by revealing to Julie that Walter Bramsby was involved with another woman.

Julie was shocked. "I don't believe it."

"But it's true, darling."

"Oh Edward."

I told her that for her sake I'd bothered to hire a detective to investigate Walter. "It's always better to be cautious, isn't it?"

Julie seemed in a daze. When she asked who the woman was, I offered a false name. I did not tell her about Claire.

Then Julie asked if I thought she still ought to marry Bramsby. "It's not as if we're engaged. At the moment he's completely free. But do you think I ought to go on with it?"

I considered the matter. I finally shrugged and said why not? I said Walter's dalliance with another woman was only temporary. I reminded Julie that she herself was in the midst of an affair. "With your sister's husband."

Julie laughed. She said she was more and more inclined to accept Walter's proposal of marriage. She said she felt he would make an adequate husband. "He's quite proper, isn't he?"

But then soon after that day Walter announced to Julie that he would not marry her. Julie was stunned. Walter refused to give any reason for his change of heart. Julie came to me in tears and told me everything. She reported that Walter seemed angry at her. He acted as if she had deceived him.

I comforted her. I said she would soon forget Walter Bramsby. "He's too boring, darling. You need a man with more vigor."

Then Mr. Cutter revealed to me that Claire had recently visited Bedford Way with the same man whose rooms she so often frequented. Mr. Walter Bramsby. "They went in and out. I'd say they were in no more than an hour. If that's of any interest to you, sir."

Interest, indeed. Now I was astonished again. How devilish Claire was. Now I understood that Claire had brought Walter to spy upon myself and Julie. She wanted Walter to see us together. Walter's response was to cancel his plans to marry Julie. The man was a mere pawn in Claire's hands. Claire had deliberately manipulated the termination of Walter's courtship to her sister. Poor Walter had played the clown for Claire's amusement.

But Julie's gaiety was soon restored. She quickly ceased to talk of Walter Bramsby. She continued to meet me in Bedford Way. Her hedonism was rampant again. We continued our games in the flat. I played the puppeteer. Now I knew that often Claire was watching us. And Claire did not know that I knew it. What a lark it was. Julie and myself on the bed while Claire watched us from the other side of that wall. On occasion I could hear Claire's movements, a scraping sound, a minor collision of a knee against the woodwork. There was never any sign of her spying when we were all together in the evening.

In Bedford Way Julie became more and more aggressive. She demanded her pleasures. She amused herself with me. And why not? It was clear to me that we all preyed upon each other. I found myself more and more obsessed with Julie. She aroused me more than Claire did. I suppose Claire was aware of that as a result of her spying. Julie teased me constantly, dominated me sexually now. I yielded to her demands. I always yielded to her demands.

And did Claire watch it all? I had no love for Julie. We used each other, exhausted each other without respite. I soon realized I disliked her intensely. I told myself she was as evil as Claire. I decided I hated both sisters. The two Fontan sisters were a pair of witches. They both enjoyed using me. I told myself I was a victim. I told myself I had to find a way to get even. I wanted vindication. I wanted revenge.

Chapter Seventeen

WHAT I DID WAS TALK to Simon Ruddle, an old acquaintance, a music hall manager, a man who looked his best in a boater and plus-fours. I said I wanted an introduction to an actress named Lily Graham. Did he know her? Yes of course he knew her, whatever did I want that one for? "She's not reliable," he said. I told him I had no concern about her reliability, I wanted the introduction as soon as possible.

And so the meeting with Lily Graham was adequately arranged by Simon Ruddle. I was determined now to have my vengeance against Claire and Julie. I went to Lily's dressing room one evening, carried my hat and cane in my hand and entered a cloud of perfume thick enough to choke a rhino. And there she was, a perfect little tart, a typical actress, blonde and pink and laughing blue eyes and delicious rosebud lips. Not much of an actress really, but a complete cocotte. "So pleased to meet you, Mr. Ransom. Shall I call you Edward? Yes, I think I shall. It's a nice name, isn't it?"

Lovely ankles in dark silk. She was amused when she learned I was Claire's husband. The laughing blue eyes moved up and down as she flirted with me. She was one of those women who flirt with men as a matter of policy. She agreed to dine with me. "Provided it's a decent place, of course. I don't like the ordinary places. I like a bit of polish, if you know what I mean."

Yes, I did know. I was overwhelmed by the perfume and her complete femininity. As was Claire, I suppose. How amusing it was. Lily's sexuality was so intense it filled the room. My mind was in a fever as I imagined her with Claire. Hot imaginings. I thought of their bodies entwined. Claire kissing her breasts, sucking her nipples, nuzzling in her nest. Claire would treat her as an hors d'oeuvre. Lily would be a delicate hors d'oeuvre for Claire. How completely clever of Claire to amuse herself with this tropical bird.

I took Lily Graham to the Ritz and she was delighted. She clapped her hands and settled her feathers. I ordered champagne. I offered a toast to her ravishing beauty. I told her every eye in the room was upon her and the blue eyes danced in response.

But it was true. The eyes of all the men were upon her. She was certainly something to look at. She flaunted her beauty at them, gazed at one and then the other, a hint of promise, a smile. She knew precisely what she had and she knew precisely what the men around her wanted.

Then she looked at me. "And you?"

"Me?"

"What do you want with me, Mr. Edward Ransom?"

"I thought we decided you would call me Edward."

"Such a nice name. And wanting what?"

She was not stupid. So often one thinks such a woman less than clever, but usually the case is otherwise. They don't go far without cleverness. Lord knows where she came from, but she now had a life of sorts. A name in the music halls, pleasant evenings with moneyed men in attendance. I could she her breasts, the glow of her skin. I wondered what she looked like naked. I sipped my champagne and lit a cigar and said I wanted to buy her.

She laughed. That sparkling music hall laugh, the blue eyes now burning. Her laughter rippled across the table. She was delighted. She sipped her champagne. She said it was lovely to find a man so honest. "You say it right out, don't you? Well, I like that. I think it's lovely. And what will you do with me after you buy me?"

How amusing she was. She knew the world. I told her I would surround her with flowers. "And then make passionate love to you. We'll make love in a bed of white roses."

Her teeth glistened as she smiled. "Now that's a fancy, isn't it? What did Claire tell you about me?"

"Nothing at all. She has no knowledge of this and I'd rather you wouldn't tell her."

"A bit of intrigue, isn't it?"

"Yes, quite."

"You're not what I imagined. Not Claire's husband. You're different."

I suppose she thought I'd be a species of poodle, combed and beribboned and quick to the beckoning. Fiery images filled my brain. I imagined Lily in my arms. That deep cleft between her breasts looked so delicious, a place to nuzzle, a place where the warm scent of her body would be intoxicating. Then I imagined her in Claire's arms. What did they do with each other? I imagined Claire making love to Lily. I imagined Lily's breasts in Claire's hands, Claire's mouth on Lily's sex. Claire would be the aggressor. My dear Claire. She would lose herself with a toy like Lily. I pictured the two women together in a feverish embrace, their mouths pulling at each other's flesh.

Then I told myself I was a fool for being so obsessed with it. I ought to have more equanimity. I chided myself for allowing my brain to become addled.

Lily persisted in questioning me. She knew I was up to something. She toyed with me. She moved to sit beside me and I adored it. Now I had her scent in my nose. Once again I said I wanted to make love to her.

Her eyes were hot as she teased me. "I prefer women, you know."

"Like my wife?"

She laughed. "She's a beauty, isn't she? Yes, like your wife."

I said I was aware of her preferences. I said I wanted her nevertheless. I said I hoped to persuade her to yield to me as a diversion. Would she be interested? For the proper sum, of course. She smiled at me. It was understood that I would pay handsomely. I did not pretend it would be anything else. She laughed and agreed when I named an exorbitant sum.

"That's quite charming."

"But sufficient?"

"Oh dear yes. It's lovely."

I thought to see her again in a few days, but she wanted to sleep with me immediately, that very night. I was taken aback but I agreed. She was amused at my surprise and asked if I found this evening inconvenient. I said not all. "But I don't think we can have the bed of white roses. We can't have that done so quickly."

She tossed her feathers as we left the Ritz. In the hansom cab she laughed and said I looked much too serious. She talked about her career. She spoke of her travels on the Continent. She said she adored the stage.

And then we arrived. She had a cluttered flat in Bloomsbury, a place filled with smells of perfume and powder and a hint of incense. Now I had a violent need. I wanted her. I took her in my arms and kissed her. I bared her breasts. I admired her pink nipples. She enjoyed exhibiting herself; she enjoyed my compliments. She was eager to be adored. She made sounds of pleasure as I sucked her nipples. When I wanted to undress her further, she laughed and refused. She unbuttoned my trousers to have a look at my tool. She toyed with it, amusing herself, delighting in my arousal. After seating herself upon a footstool, she took my root in her mouth. Her talent for sucking was immediately obvious. I was amused that a woman who preferred other women could show such passion for sucking. I withdrew from her mouth before I spent. I said I wanted her naked. "Like a nymph, my sweet. As naked as a nymph."

She teased me as she undressed for me. The gown fell, then her chemise and drawers. Finally she lay naked upon her bed wearing nothing but her dark silk stockings. I quickly stripped my clothes away and joined her. She giggled as I took her. I pulled her legs over my shoulders and penetrated her forcefully. Her eyes shone with amusement. In the end it was she who took me. She watched me spend in her grotto. She remained aloof, watching the male in his final spasms.

When at last I withdrew, I made her keep her legs apart so that I could look at her sex. It was a pretty little cunt, not much hair, the flesh pink and firm. I imagined Claire making love to it. I touched it. I wet my fingers in Lily's grotto. I went home that evening with her scent on my hand.

I did not see Lily again until two days later. We had dinner again and then we went directly to her flat. This time I questioned her about Claire but she refused to say anything of substance. She insisted I ask my wife about their affair. She said she hardly saw Claire any more. She said she disliked lengthy liaisons. I had a sudden desire to suck her sex and she was delighted. She laughed and threw her legs up as I went about it. Her sex was ravishing, succulent and warm, a delightful fruit to be sucked and nibbled. Before long she rolled over and offered me her bottom. "I think you fancy that."

Yes, of course. I teased her, amused myself with her lust. I sucked her sex from the rear, my mouth pressed against her blonde fig, my nose pressed between her bottom-cheeks. Then I tickled her rose-hole with my tongue. She quivered and said she adored it. I moved my lips back and forth between her slit and the puckered rosette of her bottom. I made her spend with my mouth on her clitoris and my finger in her fundament.

Later, as we lay upon her bed, I told Lily I wanted her to seduce my sister-in-law. "She's Claire's sister. Her name is Julie and she's quite beautiful."

Lily laughed. "Oh, what a devil you are!" She questioned me about Julie. Lily would receive a present, of course. When I named a sum, she quickly agreed. "You know how to tempt me, don't you, darling?" She said I might watch it if I liked. "From that cabinet. Won't you like that?"

I was delighted and I accepted the offer. Dear Lily took to it so easily. I wondered if she had done this sort of thing before. I suppose she had. She seemed totally at ease as we made our plans.

During the following days, the prospect of watching Lily with Julie totally occupied my mind. Finally one evening I introduced Julie to Lily in a restaurant. Lily proved to be an amazing creature. She had enormous powers of seduction and Julie was soon taken with her. In a few days Lily reported to me that Julie had agreed to visit her flat in Bloomsbury.

So it was done. The plans were made. The large cabinet in Lily's bedroom was cleared and made ready for me. When the day arrived, there I was hidden in Lily Graham's armoire. I heard them in the drawing room. I heard the soft talk, then the kisses. Before long they came into the bedroom. Julie's breasts were already bared. Lily crooned over Julie's breasts, holding them in her hands, laughing as she kissed Julie's nipples. I was in a daze of arousal. I watched the two women in their minuet, Lily undressing Julie, then Lily undressing herself and offering her breasts to Julie's mouth.

Julie moaned constantly. I realized this was the real Lily. The hunger she had for Julie was obvious. She soon had Julie upon the bed with Julie's knees pulled back to show her sex. Lily swooped down upon it. She fed upon Julie, an abandoned sucking that soon had Julie spending over and over again.

And then finally the two of them were locked in each other's arms head to toe.

I watched Julie suck Lily's blonde fig.

Julie's desire was evident enough.

* * *

Some weeks later, Claire and Julie and myself were at Prince's. We took turns dancing. We'd had a bit too much wine and both sisters had flushed cheeks. Soon the women amused themselves dancing the tango with a series of young men. I felt no jealousy. My mind was filled with images. I wondered how soon Claire would take another lover to replace Walter Bramsby. I knew that Julie was secretly seeing Lily as often as possible. I wondered if Claire still saw Lily on occasion. Had Lily told Claire about me? I doubted it.

The next day I was alone with Claire in her bedroom. Julie was out of the house, visiting Lily perhaps. I had Claire upon her bed, her knees pushed back to her breasts as I sucked her sex.

Claire teased me when she saw my hunger for it. "Be gentle, darling. I'm always afraid of you when you're famished like this."

I sucked her juices. She mewled with delight when I tongued her bottom-hole. I finally made her spend with my fingers. I stroked her grotto with my fingers while I rubbed her clitoris with my thumb. She spent twice, her face flushed and her eyes glazed.

Then suddenly Claire pushed me away. She said she knew all about my affair with Julie. "It's horrible, isn't it?" She began weeping as she told me how horrible it was.

I left her sobbing on the bed and walked out of the room.

Part Four: Edward— One Year Later

Chapter Eighteen

Chairs on the beach. I do like chairs on the beach. In the sun and silence. Three of us in wicker chairs on the beach at Biarritz. The hotel behind us, the sea in front of us, and overhead the birds in the pale blue sky.

I sit between Claire and Julie, Claire on my left, Julie on my right.

Now a breeze is stirring. Julie moves her leg. They wear wide-brimmed hats. Their bathing dresses almost completely cover their bodies.

I wear a tight wool bathing suit. Black wool. I watch the people who stroll along the beach near the water.

I have no real liking for the sea. I think people who like the sea are too romantic. They dream of exotic bungalows in the East Indies and dark-skinned girls with flowers in their hair. I prefer a hotel in Biarritz and a selection of English ladies strolling upon the beach. English ladies strolling and my two French women beside me.

Edward, you're not at all romantic. Are the women sleeping? The sun always makes me drowsy. Now I wish the beach were private and deserted. I would have the women nude on the beach. Julie's full breasts bobbing as she walks upon the sand. Claire's tight buttocks. Claire would be less modest, more poised in her nakedness. She always shaves her mound now. Her nether lips are hairless, the pink lips exposed. This morning I stroked her thighs. She lay upon our bed naked on her belly as I stroked her thighs. Then Julie entered the room already dressed for breakfast. Julie was annoyed at finding us unprepared to go downstairs with her.

She said she couldn't wait and she left. I remember her pouting.

* * *

Later in the afternoon all three of us are in Julie's room. We have connecting rooms. The two women are naked on the bed. I sit in a chair near the open window and watch them. There is music from somewhere, violins from one of the hotel gardens fronting the beach. Julie lies on her back, Claire on her side and facing Julie. Claire supports her head with her left hand. Her right hand moves slowly back and forth over Julie's belly. Then her fingers move higher and she touches one of Julie's nipples. Claire's fingers pull at the nipple. Julie closes her eyes. "I wish they wouldn't play that awful music. The trouble with Biarritz is that it's much too English." Claire pulls at the other nipple. Then her hand leaves Julie's breasts and travels down to her belly again. Now she moves her fingers into Julie's thick nest. Julie sighs and opens her legs to invite a more intimate caress. Claire begins a slow stroking of Julie's sex. She whispers in Julie's ear and Julie murmurs in response. Claire moves. Julie raises her knees. Claire moves around to kneel in front of Julie. She strokes Julie's thighs.

I look to the sea a moment and watch a bird. The bird glides, then beats its wings, then glides again. Down at the edge of the water, a man wearing a yellow boater and a black wool bathing suit strolls alone.

I look at the women again. Claire bends to Julie's sex. Julie moans. Claire's mouth is against Julie's sex. Julie's eyes are closed. Her mouth is slightly open. She makes a whispering sound as Claire makes love to her.

After a while Claire moves again. She turns her body. She positions herself over Julie, straddling Julie and facing her feet. Now Claire's mouth is on Julie's sex again. Claire's sex is over Julie's mouth. Julie raises and opens her knees wide. She strokes Claire's buttocks. Claire settles her sex upon Julie's mouth. The two women suck each other slowly as I watch them.

* * *

In the evening the sound of the surf seems louder. In our room again, I sit in one of the easy chairs. My root is out of my trousers. Julie kneels at my feet, her head bent over my lap, her lips closed over my knob. Claire lies on her side on the bed and watches us. Julie's head slowly bobs up and down as she sucks. Then Claire speaks. She talks about the people at dinner. "The men are so dull. I hate political discussions during dinner. Conversation at dinner ought to be interesting, don't you think?"

"Africa can be interesting."

My eyes are upon Julie's mouth. Claire groans with annoyance as she complains about dinner again.

* * *

All three of us are naked. Claire kneels upon the bed, her face resting on her folded arms. Her knees are apart, her bottom raised, offered, her skin milk-white.

I kneel behind her. I hold her hips as I slowly penetrate her sex. I watch my root as it slides in and out of the mouth of her grotto.

Julie sits in a nearby chair. She has one leg raised, her foot planted on the seat cushion, her sex exposed. She fingers her sex as she watches us.

I continue sliding my root in and out of Claire's open sex. My testicles jiggle against her nether-lips.

* * *

Now Julie is on her back, her legs raised, her calves resting on my shoulders as I slowly move my root in and out of her sex. I support myself with my arms. My hips move up and down. Claire sits beside us on the bed. She strokes my bottom. Then she reaches between my legs to clutch my testicles. She holds my balls as I continue pumping my root in and out of Julie's open sex.

* * *

The two women are together on the bed. Julie is over Claire, hair unbound, her face between Claire's thighs. Claire has her arms around Julie's buttocks, her mouth pressed between Julie's nether-lips. One of the women makes a sound of pleasure, but I cannot tell which one. I sit near the window with my erect penis in my hand. I slowly stroke my penis as I watch them. I watch Claire's hands as they grip Julie's buttocks. Claire's knuckles are white. Now a soft sound of sucking. The women murmur. Then suddenly a laugh in the hotel corridor as some people pass the door. I look at the ormolu clock on the mantel opposite the bed. I wonder if we ought to go somewhere else next year. I think about England as I watch Claire's hands fondle Julie's buttocks. I miss London. I want to take them dancing at Prince's again. I always like to see the sisters dancing. We shall dance at Prince's in a lovely season.

Available now

The Captive
by Anonymous

When a wealthy Enlish man-about-town attempts to make advances to the beautiful twenty-year-old debutante Caroline Martin, she haughtily repels him. As revenge, he pays a white-slavery ring £30,000 to have Caroline abducted and spirited away to the remote Atlas Mountains of Morocco. There the mistress of the ring and her sinister assistant Jason begin Caroline's education—an abduction designed to break her will and prepare her for her mentor.

Available now

Captive II
by Richard Manton

Following the best-selling novel, *The Captive*, this sequel is set among the subtropical provinces of Cheluna, where white slavery remains an institution to this day. Brigid, with her dancing girl figure and sweeping tresses of red hair, has caused the prosecution of a rich admirer. As retribution, he employs the underground organization Rio 9 to abduct and transport her to Cambina Alta Plantation. Naked and bound before the Sadism of Col. Manrique and the perversities of the Comte de Zantra, Brigid endures an education in submission. Her training continues until she is ready to be the slave of the man who has chosen her.

Available now

Captive III: The Perfumed Trap
by Anonymous

The story of slavery and passionate training described first-hand in the spirited correspondence of two wealthy cousins, Alec and Miriam. The power wielded by them over the girls who cross their paths leads them beyond Cheluna to the remote settlement of Cambina Alta and a life of plantation discipline. On the way, Alec's passion for Julie, a golden-haired nymph, is rivaled by Miriam's disciplinary zeal for Jenny, a rebellious young woman under correction at a police barracks.

Forthcoming

Captive IV: The Eyes Behind the Mask
by Anonymous

The Captives of Cheluna feel a dread fascination for the boy whose duty it is to chastise. This narrative follows a masked apprentice who obeys his master's orders without pity or restraint. Emma Smith's birching would cause a reform school scandal. Secret additions to the frenzy of nineteen-year-old Karen and Noreen mingle the boy's fierce passion with lascivious punishment. Mature young women like Jenny Woodward pay dearly for defying their master, whose masked servant also prints the marks of slavery on Lesley Hollingsworth, following *Captive II*. The untrained and the self-assured alike learn to shiver, as they lie waiting, under the caress of the eyes behind the mask.

Available now

Captive V: The Soundproof Dream
by Richard Manton

Beauty lies in bondage everywhere in the tropical island of Cheluna. Joanne, a 19-year old rebel, is sent to detention on Krater Island where obedience and discipline occupy the secret hours of night. Like the dark beauty Shirley Wood and blond shopgirl Maggie Turnbull, Jo is subjected to unending punishment. When her Krater Island training is complete, Jo's fate is Metron, the palace home of the strange Colonel Mantrique.

TITLES IN THE SHADOW LANE SERIES FROM BLUE MOON BOOKS

Available now

SHADOW LANE

In a small New England village, four spirited young women explore the romance of discipline with their lovers. Laura's husband is handsome but terribly strict, leaving her no choice but to rebel. Damaris is a very bad girl until detective Flagg takes her in hand. Susan simultaneously begins her freshman year at college and her odyssey in the scene with two charming older men. Marguerite can't decide whether to remain dreamily submissive or become a goddess.

Available now

SHADOW LANE II
Return to Random Point

All Susan Ross ever wanted was a handsome and masterful lover who would turn her over his knee now and then without trying to control her life. She ends up with three of them in this second installment of the ongoing chronicle of romantic discipline, set in a village on Cape Cod.

Available now

SHADOW LANE III
The Romance of Discipline

Mischievous Susan Ross, now at Vassar, continues to exasperate Anthony Newton, while pursuing other dominant men. Heroically proportioned Michael Flagg proves capable but bossy, while handsome Marcus Gower has one too many demands. Dominating her girlfriend Diana brings Susan unexpected satisfaction, but playing top is work and so she turns her submissive over to the boys. Susan then inspires her adoring servant Dennis to revolt against his own submissive nature and turn his young mistress over his knee.

Available now

SHADOW LANE IV
The Chronicles of Random Point

Ever since the fifties, spanking has been practiced for the pleasure of adults in Random Point. The present era finds Hugo Sands at the center of its scene. Formerly a stern and imperious dom, his persistent love for Laura has all but civilized him. But instead of enchanting his favorite submissive, Hugo's sudden tameness has the opposite effect on Laura, who breaks every rule of their relationship to get him to behave like the strict martinet she once knew and loved. Meanwhile ivy league brat Susan Ross selects Sherman Cooper as the proper dominant to give her naughty friend Diana Stratton to and all the girls of Random Point conspire to rescue a delightful submissive from a cruel master.

Available now

SHADOW LANE V
The Spanking Persuasion

When Patricia's addiction to luxury necessitates a rescue from Hugo Sands, repayment is exacted in the form of discipline from one of the world's most implacable masters. Carter compels Aurora to give up her professional B&D lifestyle, not wholly through the use of a hairbrush. Marguerite takes a no-nonsense young husband, with predictable results. Sloan finds the girl of his dreams is more like the brat of his nightmares. Portia pushes Monty quite beyond control in trying to prove he's a switch. The stories are interconnected and share a theme: bad girls get spanked!

ORDER FORM
Attach a separate sheet for additional titles.

Title	Quantity	Price
____	____	____
____	____	____
____	____	____
____	____	____

Shipping and Handling (see charges below) ____

Sales tax (in CA and NY) ____

Total ____

Name ____

Address ____

City ____ State ____ Zip ____

Daytime telephone number ____

❑ Check ❑ Money Order (US dollars only. No COD orders accepted.)

Credit Card # ____ Exp. Date ____

❑ MC ❑ VISA ❑ AMEX

Signature ____

(if paying with a credit card you must sign this form.)

Shipping and Handling charges:*

Domestic: $4 for 1st book, $.75 each additional book. International: $5 for 1st book, $1 each additional book

*rates in effect at time of publication. Subject to Change.

Mail order to Publishers Group West, Attention: Order Dept., 1700 Fourth St., Berkeley, CA 94710, or fax to (510) 528-3444.

PLEASE ALLOW 4-6 WEEKS FOR DELIVERY. ALL ORDERS SHIP VIA 4TH CLASS MAIL.

Look for Blue Moon Books at your favorite local bookseller or from your favorite online bookseller.